Heart Full of Storm

A Tropical MM Paranormal Romance of Love and Loss

JB Thomas

AETHERLYS PUBLISHING

Heart Full of Storm

A Tropical MM Paranormal Romance of Love and Loss

JB Thomas

Aetherlys Publishing

ISBN Print: 978-1-7642821-0-9

ISBN Ebook: 978-1-7642821-1-6

Interior Design and Formatting: Pagan Cat Publishing

Contents

Prologue

July 2025

Eliza Rickman's 'Pretty Little Head' keens while Rex Dutton frantically descends Grassy Hill. He holds his boyfriend's naked body close, wrapped in a frayed quilt.

He's breathing hard and tears blur his vision.

Must get away... must get away... must get away!

Big drops of rain fall, mingling with the sweat clinging to his skin as he glances over his shoulder.

Lightning fractures the night sky in a jagged burst of white, casting a sudden, blinding light that reveals figures running after him in the distance. He looks straight ahead again and begins running towards the house beyond the swaying palms—its windows glowing, music pulsing within.

"Help!" he shouts, his voice raw.

But no one hears him.

The music, the wind, the thunder—all too loud, drowning his pleas.

He stumbles barefoot towards the Queenslander. With his heel, he kicks open the wooden gate, and rushes through the threshold. Under the security light's glow, his muscles gleam and his heart pounds with a terrible density.

A high-pitched ringing begins in his left ear, causing him to stumble and almost fall. He knows he has to act now before *it* stops him.

Gently, he places the body down on the wet grass.

"I'm sorry."

He quickly removes the large platinum ring from his middle finger and slips it like an anchor onto his boyfriend's left thumb.

"I love you, Julian."

The ringing in his ear becomes so sharp, it makes his teeth hurt.

He picks up a smooth black stone and throws it as hard as he can at the window.

Glass shatters.

He then reaches into his back pocket and pulls out something. It glints in the fluorescent light.

The front door swings open and time becomes molasses.

The ringing in his ear intensifies, and he hears the roar of the ocean coming to fill him.

"Heeeyyyy!" a distorted voice shouts in anger. "What... the... fuck... are... you... doing?"

The hollow echo of urgent footsteps on pavement surge up from behind like a sudden tide, chasing the silence ahead.

"REEEEEXXXX!"

He turns his head—and takes a deep breath. A group of figures stand motionless in the yard, their faces hidden behind glimmering molten gold masks, their features fluid.

Two are running right at him, but they may as well be snails.

Beyond terror now, he puts the muzzle to his head, holds tightly to Julian's hand, and as he pulls the trigger, something louder than the gunshot shrieks.

Chapter One

JANUARY 2025

Who the hell told Satan it was okay for him to sit his ball sack down on the surface of Far North Queensland and fuck it? Wet season, my ivory gay ass! What wet season? Isn't a rainforest supposed to have, oh, I dunno, rain! This town's drier than a sinner's mouth on judgement day. Tennessee has hot days, but this humidity is ridiculous. They don't make SPF high enough for this heat.

Annoyed by the giant glowing yellow ogre in the sky and the constant bump of shoulders, I snarl under my breath and scan the area for shade. In the distance, a cluster of tall palm trees stretch their welcoming shadows across the dry ground. Beyond them, the glistening bay shimmers blue, framed by mountains dressed in dense green rainforest.

Without a moment's hesitation, I make a beeline for their cover.

I growl the Lord's name under my breath. "Where the hell am I?"

"Port Douglas," a male voice full of gravel answers.

I turn my head and pull up the brim of my enormous hat. Beside me, keeping pace, is the most beautiful guy I have ever had the pleasure of looking at. Amber eyes, tan skin, wavy black hair; he looks like a boho Clark Kent with a personality.

His accent has to be Canadian.

I push my oversized Mary Kate sunglasses back and fight not to blush, but the heat is doing me no favours. "Thank you," I say. "It's my dementia, you see. I'm not supposed to be allowed outside by myself, but nobody was watching the side gate today."

His smile reveals straight pearly whites. "Where are you from?"

"Tennessee," I say, heading towards the shade where a fortune telling booth stands.

"Ah!" He grins, walking beside me. "I was thinking Georgia with that accent. Tennessee is beautiful. Smokey Mountains, Gatlinburg, Dolly Parton's Stampede, Grand Ole Opry, and Mountain Dew."

"Where are you from?" I ask out of immediate curiosity, looking back over at him. I'm average height, and he is at least half a foot taller than me and smells of coconut and sunshine.

"Vancouver," he answers.

"Oh!" I nod, fighting my hardest not to express my excitement. "I love Vancouver. I got to walk across the Capilano Suspension Bridge, got lost at the Museum of Anthropology on purpose, felt offended that I couldn't pet a baby bear on Grouse Mountain, and cried when there wasn't enough time for a sleepover at the aquarium because we were spending another week in Whistler."

He keeps grinning. "What did you think of Whistler?"

"It has got to be the most magical place I've ever been," I answer him honestly. "I could live happily ever after there."

"I want to say I miss it," he says as he waves to a few people walking by. "We moved here when I was ten."

"Shade!" I cry, feeling the shadows embrace my wretchedness like we are old friends with many benefits. "So, what's your name? Clark Kent?"

"Clark Kent?" He crosses his strapping arms in front of his well-built chest. "Is that who you think I look like?"

I look down at what I assume are vegan friendly sandals and immaculate toenails. "If the faux leather fits..."

He cocks a manicured brow. "I like you. You're my vibe."

"I'm Julian," I tell him. "Julian Vines. Just moved here."

"Rex Dutton," he shares, extending his hand. "Been here for nine years. Nice to meet you, Julian."

I shake his bigger hand. "Is this your stall?" 'She Was Out in The Water' plays from within all that billowing material.

"Yes." He nods, giving my hand a squeeze before releasing it. "Welcome to The Oracle of the Brine."

Draped in layers of seafoam green and iridescent silver mist, his booth looks exactly like something from Ziegfeld Follies. Burnished gold lanterns hang on either side of the entrance.

Is a young Lucille Ball about to part the curtains and ask to read my palm?

"Would you like me to tell your fortune?" He leans over a small table to look at a clipboard. It is full of names with phone numbers beside each chosen time slot.

I think about it for only a second and nod. "I think I have enough cash left for a card reading."

He parts the silken threshold and gestures for me to take a seat at the round table draped in a pearlescent mermaid scale cloth. I sit down and notice an aquamarine and selenite wand resting on top of a tarot deck.

He fluffs about for a few moments.

He turns down the volume on the stereo before parking an ass capable of causing a car crash onto the chair opposite me.

He picks up a neon pink lighter and brings a flame to a bundle of mugwort. At first the dry leaves curl and blacken, crackling softly. A thin stream of smoke rises, pale and fragrant, curling in the air like a ghost's breath.

As he blows gently on the glowing tip, it flares to life with a sudden, warm-orange pulse—embers blooming like molten petals in the bundle's heart. The surface glows brighter with each breath, the burn deepening inward, illuminating the curled edges of the leaves to flickers of red and gold. He then places it in a large abalone shell. I watched the grey smoke slither through the air.

He puts the crystals aside and takes up the cards. They look traditional and well used. The illustrations remind me of Manly P Hall's work. If this is his original deck, it is worth a small fortune.

"Knock on the deck three times, ask your question out loud, shuffle them until they feel right to you, draw three, and place them on the table in the order you draw them."

He hands the cards to me. I take them and hold them between my palms, turning my gaze upwards. A string of glowing blue fairy lights twinkle back at me.

What is it I want to know?

There are many things.

I roll my eyes and knock on the deck three times. "Hello, Tarot. I'm new here. Nobody knows me except for my parents. Please, tell me, how do I find a boyfriend in a place like this?"

I put them down on the table and begin messing them up. I don't know how to shuffle to save my gay ass from a drunk kangaroo. Like Xena, I have many skills; however; I lack this one.

I give them a good messy shuffle, thinking about my question the entire time as I stack them back into a neat pile. From the top, middle, and bottom, I draw three cards, placing them in front of him in the order I pick them.

He takes the remaining cards from me and places them to the side. In the light, I admire the thick, chunky silver ring wrapped round his middle finger—shiny and weighty, though otherwise unremarkable.

I watch him turn the first card over with that large hand.

"The High Priestess." He places his index finger on her veil. "You enjoy exploring depths and currents others fear. Hidden knowledge is going to play a key role in your life. You've got powerful instincts, and your inner voice has always been your loudest ally. Don't ignore it. Speaking the truth, being up front and honest about what you want; these are the tools that will forge a meaningful connection with someone."

I nod my head.

He's making sense.

Speaking the truth has rendered my circle small. In fact, my circle is non-existent.

He smirks as he turns the next card over.

"The Lovers. I'm not surprised. This is what you asked for and this is the card of love and union, the merging of two paths, two souls. You are being guided, so follow your heart wherever it may lead you. An authentic connection is going to present itself, and you will have the choice to align and commit."

I'm a little freaked out. A standard tarot deck has seventy-eight cards, so the chances of me pulling this one at this time is strange.

He flips over the third card. "Wow. All three of your cards are major arcana. Something destined is happening here."

The Magician!

"Who better to help you manifest a relationship than The Magician? He is the ultimate manifestor. You have all the tools you need to create your desired outcome. You seem like the type of person who always gets what he wants."

I almost snort as I take off my hat and remove my sunglasses.

I like to see people's eyes widen as I turn mine on them.

He didn't disappoint.

My irises are obsidian, but when the light hits them, they're the colour of red wine.

He blinks and looks back down at the cards.

He's not wrong in his assumption.

No matter how long it might take me, I always reach my goals.

I am like a serpent with heat vision. I focus on the object of my desire and I activate lasers.

He pulls a fourth card from the deck and he assumes a more mysterious and slightly startled appearance.

"What?" I ask.

"The Two of Cups." He places the card down on top of The Lovers. "This is the soulmate or mutual attraction card. It signifies emotional connection, harmony, and partnership. I believe you're going to find yourself a boyfriend."

"So, I'm going to bump into him, and he will immediately fall in love with my quirky personality?"

"This relationship will be deeply emotional and spiritually significant. You need to trust yourself, align with your heart's truth, and just be your funny self. Yes. I believe you've... you will bump into this guy."

His words have me smiling. "Thanks for the reading, Rex. It's been enlightening." I reach for my bag to pull out my wallet, but he stops me by placing his large hand on my slender wrist.

"My gift," he says, gently squeezing my wrist. "Welcome to Port Douglas, Julian Vines."

"Thank you." I meet his honey gaze.

He withdraws his hand, turns to his left, and slips a business card from between the pages of a tea leaf reading book. As he hands it to me, I'm immediately struck by the luxurious cardstock—elegant gold script swirling above silver bubbles that shimmer like seafoam.

Oracle of The Brine

Text me rain or shine

All we have is an endless spiral of time

7777 5656

I almost burst out laughing.

So ridiculous; it's cute!

His phone number also reminds me of a sequence of angel numbers.

I'll do a quick Google search later and find out.

If that's what they are, he's a genius.

"Send me a text later," he says. "I think you should come with me to yoga."

I love yoga.

I'm not very good at it, but I enjoy how it makes me feel. Plus, I like the music.

And since this handsome guy is inviting me to text him, it feels impolite to refuse.

"Thank you." I hold up his card. "And thank you for the informative welcoming gift. I enjoy yoga, so be on the lookout for my text."

"Cool!" He grins. "Now I got to call all these people and tell them how to fix their lives, which they will ignore, and complain about later."

"Yeah." I get to my feet. "But it keeps them coming back for more."

He chuckles. "That it do."

With his business card in my hand, I laugh and leave his booth as he turns up 'Tarzan Boy'. I pull out my phone and type in the numbers.

They are angel numbers!

7777 is a clear sign you are on the cusp of a profound spiritual awakening and 5656 means you're on the right path in life and a fresh start is coming.

I program his phone number into my mobile.

Rex (Boho Clark Kent) Dutton.

I've just made a friend.

#goals!

Chapter Two

NOVEMBER 2025

DYAN is singing 'Looking For Knives' from my stereo on the shelf above the toilet.

I catch myself staring at the ugly vertical pinkish cut etched down the centre of my chest. The scar marks the incision, where a surgeon cracked open my sternum, removed my broken heart and replaced it with a stranger's.

I squeeze a nickel size amount of rose scented holistic scar gel into my palm and massage the cool liquid over my scar.

Four months have passed since my heartquake—and Rex's suicide. The never ending echoes of my screams linger like phantoms around the misty edges of my mind. No amount of therapy or medication is going to stop them haunting me.

With a deep sigh, I line up the nine prescription pills, each a daily reminder that I'd likely be swallowing them for the rest of my life.

I do my best to hold back the tears threatening to spill from my eyes. When I think I have no more tears left, I surprise myself with another flash flood.

I lace my hands over my chest and fiddle with the large silver ring Rex must have placed around my left thumb because I'd woken up with it on.

Lub-dub. Lub-dub. Lub-dub.

My reflection blurs, the mirror's surface shifting as if I'm staring out a ship's porthole at the sea.

This can't be real.

Lub-dub. Lub-dub. Lub-dub.

There appear to be mountains in the distance, but they're getting bigger and much closer.

Lub-dub. Lub-dub. Lub-dub.

A monstrous wave is coming right at me, and I can feel the rumble of its approach under my feet.

Lub-dub. Lub-dub. Lub-dub.

I close my eyes against the vision.

Rex...

I jerk—my whole body tensing—when a powerful hand grips my shoulder.

My eyes snap open, but the mirror reflects only my wide-eyed gaze and the closed bathroom door behind me.

Lub-dub. Lub-dub. Lub-dub.

I am alone.

The mirror is just a mirror.

Lub-dub. Lub-dub. Lub-dub.

Is taking so much medication messing with my head in other ways now? My doctor warned me that there could be all kinds of strange side effects.

Stepping out of the bathroom, I walk over to my dresser and reach for the small matchbox. My moisturised fingers tremble slightly as I strike a match and light a white prayer candle. The flickering flame illuminates his framed photograph, his handsome face smiling back at me from behind the glass.

"I miss you so much."

Memories.

I'm in so much pain and so heavily medicated; I don't know how much time has passed. To me, it feels like everything has just happened.

I remember begging them to let me see his body, so I can say goodbye, so I can convince myself that all of this is real, but they have already buried him.

I didn't get to say goodbye.

The Duttons tell me they would have refused my request.

They want me to remember the man who carried me through a storm in his arms—not to be haunted by the sight of a disfigured corpse on a metal slab.

A knock at my door brings me back.

"Are you dressed, sweetheart?"

"Almost," I answer.

"I don't mean to rush you, but we don't want to be late."

"I'll be down in a just a few."

"We'll be waiting."

My stepmother's retreating footsteps grow fainter.

Apparently, tonight is astrologically auspicious. The Duttons are holding a Dark Moon Ceremony. It is a deeply spiritual and special ritual for them.

They want me to be a part of it because Rex had loved me and they still consider me a part of their family because of his love.

Mrs Dutton had told me to write a letter addressing his spirit. I'm supposed to read it aloud and then place it into a consecrated flame, but I'm not sure I'll be allowed to read it.

My words are brutal and angry.

"Of course," I say, dressing myself in front of his illuminated photo. "Of course, I'd have a heart attack while getting pegged for the first time."

There's evidence I suffered a heart attack during sex.

Did he think he killed me?

Speculation swirls that this might be why Rex took his own life.

I don't buy that bullshit for a second.

My memory might be fucked, but I know him—he'd never pull a Romeo like that. He'd have made damn sure I got all the help I needed.

Tears sting my eyes.

It all feels wrong. So painfully, impossibly wrong.

"Never in a billion years, Rex..."

Even if I could look eons into the future, I still don't think I would have seen this meteor striking me.

I put my hand on my chest, draw in a trembling breath, and slowly let it out.

Lub-dub. Lub-dub. Lub-dub.

Chapter Three

FEBRUARY 2025

We move in unison under the shade sail. I can hear the waves crashing against the shore and the instructor reminds us to try and blend our breathing with the tide's rhythm.

Rex's form is powerful and practiced while I'm struggling to keep my hands from trembling against the wooden floor and toppling balls over ass onto him.

Downward Dingo has me staring at the back of his head, while fulgurite wind chimes tinkle around the circular raised platform. The sound is ethereal, almost like wind whispering through ancient glass. A soft, shimmering tone. The ghost of the lightning strike that formed them.

I've been accompanying him to Aetherlys for a few weeks now.

He got me in on a three-day visitor's pass, but I asked my parents to pay for a membership. They were more than happy if it got me out of the house and around people.

Aetherlys reminds me so much of Ferngully. Ten minutes south of Port Douglas, the resort lies tucked away within the dense embrace of the rainforest. Perched atop a towering bluff, the retreat commands sweeping views of the Coral Sea and the surrounding mountains.

The air carries the scent of salt and earth, mingling with the crisp, green fragrance of the forest. Sunlight filters through the emerald canopy, casting dappled shadows over the winding path that leads to its secluded retreat.

The private beach blows my mind. It's a paradise where the rainforest truly meets the sea. Hidden from the mundane world, it is a secluded New Ager's dream.

A large quartz singing bowl dings and brings me back to my body.

Our instructor reminds us that each breath is a precious gift from Source and then she finishes the class by blessing the rest of our day.

I follow Rex's lead and clean my mat using a sweet-smelling liquid in a plain spray bottle and cotton cloth. Afterwards, I follow him through a haze of sweet sage and down the stairs into the café.

"And another thing," I hiss, being mindful to use my indoor voice, while waiting on a Mood Ring Tea—a blend of Greek saffron, sage, St John's Wort, and Cypriot honey. "Can we talk about the mosquitoes? What the hell is up with them? Are they on steroids or are they some mutated monstrosity from Satan's nut sack? When I got bitten back home, I'd get the occasional little red bump, but these fuckers leave bruises. Look at my ankle. This is from last night. That spray I bought is useless. I think they're immune."

"I'll make you something to keep them away." Rex chuckles, passing me my tea. "Aussie mosquitoes have a thing for Americans. It is all that high fructose corn syrup still in your bloodstream."

I roll my eyes, taking a sip. The sweet flavour prances across my tastebuds and I close my eyes. Delicious!

He leads me across marble tiles to a table near the three tier swimming pool, and we sit across from each other. Even though I've been coming here three days a week for the past seven weeks, I still can't get over how expansive the property is. It seems to stretch and wind on endlessly, with a mix of private treatment rooms and villas where guests stay for days or even weeks at a time.

"I've booked you for a Raindrop Technique today," he says, blowing on his tea. "It starts in about ten minutes."

I stare across the table at him. He was talking about this earlier. "You did?"

He nods. "It is a perk for new members."

"And what exactly is this raindrop technique?"

He places his mug down and leans forward, resting his arms on the tabletop. "I think you're going to love it. It is so relaxing. Basically, high grade essential oils are being dropped along your spine and then massaged into your skin."

"And this is supposed to do what?"

"Reduce stress, boost your immune system, ease muscle tension. Since you started coming to yoga with me, I've noticed you've not been massaging your lower back as much after the gym."

I think about it. I guess he's right. My lower back isn't bothering me as much. I hurt my lower back a few years ago when helping my stepmom with our Christmas tree. I've hated Christmas ever since. "How long?"

"Depending on what messages may come through for you from the aethers, forty-five minutes to an hour." He gives me a playful wink.

I blink. "Messages? Aethers? You mean like spirit guides or angels?"

He nods. "It could be both."

"They're probably going to tell me to get off my ass and get my shit together. What will you be doing while I'm being rained on?"

"I'll be having an Egyptian Emotional Clearing done. Apparently, I still have some childhood trauma to work through."

I just look at him for a few silent seconds and he taps the top of my bare foot with the bottom of his.

Ah! He's joking. "And what is that?" I ask him.

"Practicing deep breathing and visualisation. I will go on a guided journey through my subconscious. I will receive an application of oils infused with higher vibrational energies to my chakras. This will release emotional blockages and align me with my higher self."

Oils infused with higher vibrational energies? Do they have some kind of Hadron Collider hidden around here for that? Is CERN involved? I have so many questions, but there are only so many seconds in a minute, and my attention span is already waning. "Interesting," I say, cocking a brow and speaking in a nasal tone. "Very interesting, Rex."

"Trust me," he says, rising from the table. "You're going to love this. Suzannah is the best. You're in excellent hands."

He leads me across a wooden bridge, the pond below teeming with blue lotus flowers and large goldfish in every hue.

We pass a raised dais; people sprawl on mats, absorbed in the sounds of crystal singing bowls. An orange haired woman chants about how the ocean is our mother and that we better respect her authority.

We walk the winding path between a few private villas and approach what appears to be an outdoor reception area. A young woman stands behind the counter, typing away at a tablet. Upon hearing our approach, she looks up and greets us warmly.

"Hi, Rex!" She steps around the counter. "We've got you and Julian all booked in and ready. I'll escort you to your treatment cabins."

Rex nods. "Thanks, Tania."

She slightly bows her head to him and leads the way down a cobblestone path between towering fern trees.

I lower my sunglasses and lean closer to whisper, "Did she just bow?"

"It's something some do here," he answers in a hushed tone. "Some people here worship the divinity within each person, though this practice is rare now."

I keep my confusion in check. I've been attending classes for a while now, and I have seen no one bow to him before. "Oh," I say, unsure of how to respond, deciding to let it slide. If it's something some people do, who am I to question it?

A flutter of Ulysses fly in front of us. A shifting cascade of living sapphires, rising and dipping, catching the light. They're beautiful. I never tire of seeing them.

"Here we are," she says, stopping between two cabins. "Julian to the left and Mr..." she clears her throat. "Sorry, I think I swallowed a bug. You're in this one, Rex."

"See you in a bit." He flashes white teeth. "Have fun."

I nod, giving him a small wave. I walk up the wooden ramp and step inside. Tania gently shuts the door behind me.

The skylight above bathes the space in soft, natural light. Essential oils perfumes the air, and ocean waves play in the background. In the centre stands a plush massage table, draped with white linens. Beside it, a small shelf holds a collection of essential oils that cost more than my new scooter. A large painting of a female shape illuminated by light through water hangs on the wall at the head of the bed.

A friendly knock and an older blond woman steps inside. She greets me with a warm smile and a wave. "Hello. I'm Suzannah. You're here for the Raindrop Technique, yes?"

I nod my head in response to her question. "Yes. I'm Julian Vines."

"Did Tania give you the Client History Form and the Release and Indemnity Form?"

I shake my head. "No."

"She's new. Still a little nervous. I'll get those for you. Please make yourself comfortable, and I'll be right back."

She goes back out, and I take the chair at the table in the corner.

A strange feeling settles over me, but I shake it off. This is an unfamiliar experience, and I want to see what's going to happen. Even if this whole thing turns out to be a colossal waste of my precious time, at least I'm out of the heat. Just as a yawn creeps up on me, the familiar friendly knock comes at the door, and Suzannah steps back inside.

"Here we go," she says, walking over and handing me a clipboard and pen. "Fill this out while I get a few things ready. I picked up some vibes. What sounds would you like? Whales? Harp? Thunder..."

Vibes? "Harp," I answer, glancing down at the form in my hand. To my knowledge, I'm free of allergies and illnesses. I suffer from occasional lower back pain and sleepless nights.

I barely tick any of the boxes. If people tick a lot of these boxes, they may as well invest in a coffin and get buried. I sign the Release Form and place the clipboard down on the table. "Done."

She sits down across from me and begins reviewing my paperwork. "Okay, you're an easy one, then."

That's me. Shallow as a puddle. Skip me and fuck on.

"Please remove your shirt, and lie down on your stomach."

I do as she requests and make myself comfortable.

"So, Julian, what I am going to do is drip essential oils along your spine and gently feather them in."

"Feather?" I ask. "You use feathers?"

"No!" She genuinely laughs. "Feathering is a light massage technique where my fingertips and the pads of my hands gently stroke the skin with brief pressure. It will feel soft like a feather."

"Ah!" I allow my face to sink into the memory foam pillow. "I get it."

Silver strumming of a Celtic harp fills the space, and the first few drops of oil on my neck startle me, but the scent quickly fills the air—and it's divine.

"What's that?" I ask.

"Valiant," she replies. "It's a balancing oil that supports energy and well-being. Did you know Celtic warriors used plant extracts for courage before heading into battle?"

"No. Am I about to enter a battle?"

"You're alive. Every day spent in this world is a battle."

I'm not arguing with that.

"Like Valiant, we need courage. But armour helps, too. Valiant is a shield we can put on—it protects our energy field. Keeps the psychic vampires away."

The tips of her fingers feather along my spine, and I feel my eyelids growing heavier.

"Relax. It's okay if you fall asleep. That means the treatment is doing what it needs to do for you."

Suzannah dripped a few more drops on the back of my neck, the scent of basil and oregano settling in, and with it, I let myself drift deeper into relaxation, wondering how Rex's treatment is going next door.

Is that Suzannah humming along with the harp?

My eyelids are so heavy I can't bring myself to open them to have a look and see. If it is her, her voice is beautiful. I'm going to walk out of this treatment room smelling like pizza.

"Someone is trying to come through..." her voice interrupts my vision of a Pizza Hut arcade I once saw in some 80s magazine my dad hoarded.

"Oh! That's my inner drag queen. Don't let her get within earshot. She reads."

Chapter Four

The Dutton's home, perched high above the township, crowns the summit.

Sleek glass walls, natural stone accents, and timber finishes, while wide verandahs wrap around the structure, offering views of the Coral Sea and surrounding rainforest. During the day, natural light fills the open-plan layout, thanks to skylights, floor-to-ceiling windows, and sliding glass doors opening to a sprawling outdoor oasis. Polished timber floors and soaring ceilings amplify the airy ambiance, while louvered windows and ceiling fans keep the interiors cool and comfortable with a constant flow of air that smells of rosy amber and never having to give a fuck about looking at price tags.

"Welcome, welcome," Rex's father, Clive Dutton, greets us at the front door, pulling me into a big bear hug. "Thank you so much for coming. We are so glad you could make it."

I can't help but smile as I hug him back. He's always been very kind and welcoming to me whenever Rex brought me home with him.

"Thank you," I whisper.

He holds me a few seconds longer before letting go and immediately shakes my dad's hand and kisses my stepmother on the cheek.

"Please, please come inside and make yourselves at home," he says, ushering us to enter.

Stepping into what I jokingly call the lobby, I spot Rex's mom coming down the staircase.

Alexandra Dutton is wearing a gorgeous black and gold kaftan that flutters around her graceful figure. She strolls right up to me and pulls me into a sweet-scented embrace. It's a heart-to-heart hug. She then cradles my face between her soft palms and places a kiss between my brows. "Welcome, sweetheart," she says, looking me over. "You look well and rested. I'm so happy you are here with us. Thank you for coming. It means the world."

I do my best to smile, fiddling with Rex's ring on my thumb. "Before things get started," I say, meeting her gaze, trying my very best not to look like I'm about to have another mental breakdown. "Do you think I could sit in Rex's room for a little while? I just need to—"

She interrupts me by placing her warm palm against my smooth cheek. "Of course you can." She leans forward and kisses my other cheek. "You are always welcome here."

I smile, holding back the deluge. "Thank you."

She gently pats my cheek and winks; her eyes are wet with unshed tears. The wink is an exact mirror of Rex's. Now I know where he got it from.

"I will come and get you before we start."

I nod, giving my parents a little wave before making my way towards the staircase that will take me to my dead boyfriend's bedroom.

Chapter Five

APRIL 2025

Well, fuck me diagonally with a broken cognac bottle!

Reality backhands me harder than a menopausal nun swinging a ruler. Here I've been walking around like an ignorant idiot, thinking I'm friends with hippy-dippy Superman, but it turns out he isn't who I think he is.

He isn't just a fortune teller making a killing at the Sunday market, wearing hemp shirts, cotton genie pants, messiah sandals, and always smelling of sunshine and coconut. He's someone else entirely.

An alcoholically bamboozled Tania is rambling about how great Rex's parents are for creating Aetherlys and hiring her as a permanent part-time receptionist. She's so shitfaced she doesn't even notice the seriously fucked up look on my own—or maybe she's forgotten who she's talking to.

The poor girl's thicker than two short planks, dumber than dogshit, a muppet, a drongo, a tit, and a multitude of other Aussie slang I can't think of. I'm also not too sure if I'm using them properly, nor do I give two flying fucks if I'm not.

Three months of accompanying him to yoga.

Three months of meeting and hanging out at different venues.

Everyone knows who he is.

Everyone but me!

Is this whole goddamn town in on this conspiracy?

Oh, take a gander, mate. There goes the noodle American.

"Tania." I deadpan. "Not that you'll remember any of this tomorrow, but we will have an extensive come-to-Jesus when you're sober."

I excuse myself from her slurred waffling and flee the pub. Overhead, the dark sky reverberates with distant thunder as I watch the light show over the hill. My eyes sting, and I feel like my nose is about to run. I really thought I'd made a friend. Was this some kind of joke? Was I some sort of social experiment?

I'll just go home and hideaway until my college courses start and only go out on Sundays when I know exactly where he'll be at.

I turn and gaze through the window and I can see Tania lowering her phone from her ear. She looks like she just got dumped.

My cell phone chimes from my pocket and I pull it out. It's a text from Rex.

> *Where are you?*

Did she call him?

I type back.

> *Walking to the Sugar Wharf to jump.*

He doesn't respond, so I just assume Nelstro is fucking up again. They're as reliable as a broken condom.

I'm nowhere near the Sugar Wharf and I take off at a leisurely gait down Macrossan and cut across Wharf into Market Park. Palm trees rustle in the breeze, their fronds fluttering like nervous hands as if sensing the shifting pressure in the air.

He's already waiting for me.

So, she had texted him.

I immediately see the subtle tension in his sexy jaw betraying his usual calm, confident demeanour. He looks at me like he knows exactly what I've been told, and for a moment that feels like forever, we stand in awkward silence.

A strange constellation slowly disappears behind the gathering clouds, its jagged shape resembling a lightning bolt over the waves.

"So," I finally say, stepping closer, crossing my arms as lightning spears the sea beyond the white walls behind him. "Your parents own the retreat."

He sighs, running a hand through his hair as thunder booms across the deep. "I was going to tell you."

"Were you?" My words come out sharp and stabby. "Or was I supposed to be treated like a hit and run? Because it feels great being hit head on and sent flying through the air like a fuckin' wallaby."

"It's not like that," he says, his tone annoyingly calm but firm as stone. "I wanted to see who you are—how you treat me—without knowledge of my family, without the privilege. People have... used and hurt me before."

A bitter laugh escapes me. I'm nothing like that. My parents don't live lavishly, but they live comfortably. I'd only wanted a friend I could hang out with and trust.

"So, this has been some kind of test? To see if I'd pass your little 'good person' criteria? As if I'm some kind of gold digging hussy. Has everyone given me their final scores? Do I get to move on to the next round? Is there a certificate or a diploma? Oh, a medal. I think this is medal worthy. I'd love a medal, Rex, so I can bounce it off your fucking forehead."

"Julian, that's not what I—" He stops, visibly struggling to find the right words to say because the thin ice he's standing on is cracking under his feet. "Look, I don't want my luck of birth defining how you see me. I do work. I make my own money. You've seen how full my schedule is at the market. I don't want this disastrous enlightenment from a booze loosened tongue to change what we've built."

"I don't give a shit about your parent's money. I don't give a shit about your dollars. If I want coins, I'll get a job or ask my parents. You didn't trust me enough to just be honest. I've always been honest. I'm a heinous bitch. I'm a bony cunt. I'm there at the drop of a bear and I'm pretty fucking consistent, too. I also bought those oils and did a sound bath with you. At least the chorus of annoying cicadas were in tune. That guy hummed and sang off key for an hour. AN HOUR, Rex! I wanted to see the earth burn, but I tolerated it because I thought we were friends. Also, are your parents tone deaf? Why the fuck did they even hire him?"

His eyes soften. "You're right. I should have been up front with you. I fucked up."

Mine widen. This is the first time I'd ever heard him cuss.

He hesitates, then steps closer, his deep voice quieter. "I care about you. I've not felt this way about someone since my wombat wobbled towards freedom."

His softness catches me off guard. I blink, my self-righteous anger faltering.

"I like you, Julian. A lot. You're crazy. You're funny. If nobody has anything nice to say, you pat the empty seat beside you. But you're also honest, kind where it matters, and open to exploring new things. I'm never bored when you're around."

For a moment, I just stare at him, my feelings tangled between hurt and something warmer, squishier. The sincerity and emotions in his eyes and voice disarming me. I'm not sure how to stay mean and bitchy with someone being so damn nice and apologetic. It's a magic I don't understand. Fucking Canadian!

"Rex," my anger dissipating. "You should've trusted me. Now I just feel awkward."

"I know. And I'm asking you to allow me to earn back your trust."

He reaches over and takes my hand, and I don't pull it away. I command my inner unicorn to retract his forehead sword. "I'm probably going to make your existence hell for a few days."

He smiles, his warm grip on my hand steady. "Fair enough. Does this mean you'll go out with me?"

I feel myself beginning to grin. "You really know how to complicate things, don't you?"

"I prefer to think of it as keeping life interesting."

He squeezes my hand and pulls me into a tight hug. I wrap my arms around him and close my eyes. It looks like my tarot reading has manifested.

"Are you hungry?" he asks, not letting me go yet.

I breathe him in. He smells of amber and roses.

"I could go for a masala chai and citrus tart."

Hand in hand, we walk back towards Macrossan as lightning flickers behind us.

Chapter Six

NOVEMBER 2025

Like a vampire, I stand in the open doorway, unable to cross its frame.

The rose quartz lamp glows beside his bed, and the air holds a faint trace of his scent. It lingers like a kiss that will never come, a deep longing for something forever lost.

His bedroom has its own private balcony, a walk-in wardrobe bigger than my bedroom, and a spa-like en-suite with a freestanding tub—where we had bathed together, warm water and soft laughter rising like steam as we watched the horizon fade into twilight. Now, the silence of that space feels too loud, as if the walls themselves remember what I'm slowly beginning to forget.

Realising my tight grip on the doorjamb has turned my knuckles white, I force myself to let go, and step through, taking hesitant steps towards his bed. The doona is smooth, looking freshly made, untouched by all the time that has passed.

All I want to do is sink into it, close my eyes, and escape—if only for a second. But I'm too afraid to close my eyes. Afraid I might hear him. The thought of opening my eyes, only to find him not beside me will destroy me.

I take in a deep breath, unsure if I'll ever smell the faint remnants of him again, trying my best to preserve it in my memory before it fades away forever.

I startle at the heavy thump behind me.

Turning around, I see a book on the floor, having fallen from his dresser.

I walk over, kneel, and pick it up.

Another sound.

A metallic sound against tile.

A gold key.

I grab it.

It has the number 7 inscribed on it.

The title of the book is *The Luminous Path* by Sirena Solis. I turn it over and shake it a few times. Nothing else falls out. On opening the cover to the title page, I see the author has signed it.

To Rex,
Thank you for coming to see me. I see great things for you. May your path always be
luminous, you beautiful boy.
Sirena

At the sound of approaching footsteps, I slip the key into my front pocket.

I quickly place the book back on the dresser amid a collection of trophies, then stand there, pretending to be lost in thought.

Thankfully, the footsteps go in another direction.

Wait.

Why am I so nervous?

Why am I caught up in the moment like this?

I have nothing to be nervous about. I've done nothing wrong.

A book just fell. That's all.

But how did it fall?

I turn my head, looking at it.

It's not a light read.

Even though the windows are open, I haven't felt a gust strong enough to blow it off.

A chill prickles down my spine.

The hair on the back of my neck stands up, and goosebumps break out along my arms.

Someone is behind me.

A breath against the back of my left ear.

I squeak and whip my head around, eyes wide.

"Rex?"

Nobody.

Gazing around the room, I expect to see a shadow where a shadow shouldn't be, but there's nothing. I am alone.

"Rex?" I whisper.

A soft knock at the door almost has me falling over. I turn my head back.

Alexandra!

How long has she been standing there?

She looks stunning, but somehow diminished now that I'm really looking at her.

In her trademark soft voice, she asks me, "Is there anything of Rex's you'd like to keep, Julian?"

Keep? Why is she asking me this? I'm not blood.

I shake my head. "I... I don't know... maybe this book?"

"Of course. How about I put together a few things and I'll drop them off at your place later this week," she says, smiling at me.

I don't know what to say. These were her son's belongings. I've no right to them, even though I am nervously twirling his silver ring around on my thumb.

"If you feel I deserve something..." I'm not sure what it is I'm trying to say.

"It isn't about deserving, dear," she says, stepping into the room and walking towards me, high heels clacking on tile. "You have been and will now forever be a part of this family." She takes me by my hands and gently squeezes them. "Let's go downstairs. We're about to begin in just a few moments. That's plenty of time for you to have a nibbly and something to drink."

I allow her to take my hand and guide me from the room. I glance back over my shoulder, eyeing the book and remembering the key in my pocket.

Chapter Seven

May 2025

While driving down the Captain Cook Highway from Port Douglas to Cairns, I put the air conditioning on full blast as 'Great Southern Land' plays from the speakers. The Coral Sea churns in a murky, restless shade, while waterfalls cascade alongside the road—newly formed by the torrential rains of a tropical low that lacked the big dick energy to grow into a cyclone.

Praise the gods!

There's no way I could have handled a cyclone. Just the thought of being without power and water for days is enough to send me into a homicidal spiral.

Godzilla might as well rise from the abyss and finish us with a blast of atomic breath. Which, of course, knowing my luck, he'd miss me on purpose.

"That was 'Great Southern Land' by Icehouse. I'm here with local author and instigator Jonah Brett Thompson. Now you were saying earlier you're a Gemini. I am an astrology junkie. I love getting a good reading. What is it about Geminis that lights fires in people's colons?"

"You know how we Geminis are. We walk into a room, stir the pot, immediately disassociate from the situation we create, and bounce. Someone then asks, 'Where did that demon twink go?' I've slithered behind the curtain, now sitting on the sill listening to them talk crap about me while another is like, 'Oh, Bobby! I didn't mean to kiss him that hard. I didn't know that tongue of his would touch my heart like that.' I nearly gagged, mawmaw. And, of course, I'm sun beaming through my Lemurian Contact Cloud going: 'Did I do that? Did I say that? Am I the villain? Me?' And then I violently pull aside the curtain and shout, 'AND THEN?' Just to hear them all scream in holy terror. Ugh! Us gay people. I swear. We Geminis are divine Karma. Tell me, when have you ever done something that has made you feel guilty."

"Just last week."

"And who came strolling all up into your business and left you begging for a bailout?"

"Um... ah! A Gemini!"

"There you go. Satan, in his madness, broke God's mirror, and we, as Geminis, are the resulting shards. What you give us, we direct right back at you with divine clarity. Don't start nothing with a Gemini, won't be nothing from a Gemini."

"How do you feel when a Pisces refers to you Geminis as demonic trash pieces?"

"Oh, hunny, that's our love language. They be flirting real hard with poetry like that. That kind of talk makes me want to get naked and explore just how demonically trashy I can be."

Rex laughs and turns the volume down. "Do you think I'm a demonic trash piece?"

I shake my head, not really paying attention and pull out my phone and scroll to the photo we'd taken earlier at Rex's Lookout. The two of us are smiling as rain clouds creep in from the sea. He'd confessed it was one of his favourite views, not just because they share names.

Several local YouTubers in the Daintree area report multiple UFO sightings in the area. There're rumours of a large phantom black pig that likes to run out in front of flash cars and explodes on impact into a cloud of dust.

The local rag reported a yowie sighting last week. Big hairy fuck ran out in front of some poor cane farmer, scaring the shit down his legs.

Glancing over at Rex, I can't help but ask, "What oils are you wearing?"

He smells good enough to lick.

"Acceptance and Surrender," he says, turning off the radio with a tap. "Maggie told me these are the best blends for me to wear right now—Mercury's in retrograde."

"Ah," I reply with a knowing nod. "Mercury in the lemonade. Bad news. I hear poisoning is a terrible way to go."

He smirks and reaches across to flick his finger under my chin, but I dodge his obvious attack in time.

"Eyes on the road," I tease, earning a chuckle.

He eases the car down from 80 to 60 while we pass through Ellis Beach. "We're still feeling the effects of Cyclone Jasper here." He points out the window.

It's true—three stoplights along the way because of ongoing repairs in the range. The massive rockslide happened long before my arrival. I still can't get over the size of the boulders. I can't help but imagine the thunderous roar they must've made. Dirt, trees, and stones falling from such heights must have sounded like the world was ending for anyone living in those units. Just a few more meters, and the mountain would have buried them.

"We should do the Wangetti Trail," he suggests, speeding back up to 80. "It goes from here to Palm Cove."

I tilt my sunglasses down. "We can tackle that in June when it's cooler."

"I'll plan it." He laughs. "We can rent a cabin on the beach here and go swimming in the net."

Yeah, nah. My ass isn't getting into any pool of water in this region. There are a million critters lurking that can end a human in two seconds. Crocodile snatches you in its jaws—your leg flies one way, your head soars in another. Nope. Absolutely not. "That sounds fun." I smile, glancing his way.

The thought of staying on the beach, listening to waves whisper through the screens, and cuddling up next to him sounds like heaven. "Let's do it."

He reaches over and takes my hand in his, slowing down to stop at a red light. I'm about to ask him a question when something smacks the passenger-side window.

I yelp and whip my head around to see a small crack in the glass.

Blood, or what looks like it, smears the tinted glass.

"What the hell?" I ask, leaning closer and peering down. "Was that... a bird?"

"Do you see anything?" he asks, glancing over with concern.

I shake my head. "No, and I'm not rolling the window down—just in case it won't go back up. Whatever it was, must've rolled under the truck."

"Shit," he hisses under his breath. "I'm sorry."

I turn to look at him. "What? This wasn't your fault. You have no control over a pigeon pulling a 9/11."

The look on his face tells me I'd said that aloud and not in my head.

I'm unsure if it's my dark joke or the look of horror on my face at realising my mistake, but it sets him off.

He's laughing so hard; he has to keep wiping at his eyes.

We end up getting honked at from behind because we've not noticed the light had turned green.

Should I share with him that 9/11 was an inside job?

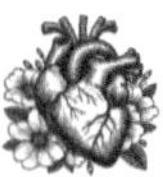

While ordering, the drinks dispenser decides to stop working. We both watch the poor girl bounce from machine to machine. Nothing!

While the frazzled assistant apologises to us and all the customers in line, the popcorn maker dies on the spot. The colourful appliance sputters and groans before falling silent.

Another flustered employee smacks it as hard as she can and then kicks the shit out of it. The poor thing only rumbles and lets out a sad hiss.

And if that's not bad enough, Wicked cuts out right as Elphaba is about to nail the last note in 'Defying Gravity.'

"Ah, ya cunt!"

The entire auditorium descends into discord and loud swearing.

Of course, I burst out laughing. Not a single soul gives a shit that kids are in attendance. People paid to hear the wicked witch's battle cry, and they feel cheated.

I love how cunt doesn't just mean a vagina. Cunt also means feral children, a best friend, a stalled engine, a life partner, a kinked garden hose, the Lego you step on, a biting green ant, the tow bar you just shattered your shin on. The uses are endless. Cunt is truly Australia's greatest noun.

The Northern Territory loves it so much, they made it a beloved slogan.

Amidst all the chaos, we look at each other and leave.

Our walk along the esplanade isn't much better. A group of Chinese tourists is chatting peacefully when, out of nowhere, an ear-splitting cacophony erupts—a horde of curlews swoops in like banshees and chases the group off in a screaming frenzy.

We try three different ice cream shops, but every single one has the same problem: the refrigeration units are down. Each tub of ice cream has melted into sad, colourful puddles.

Staff look spooked.

"It is the oddest fucking thing," the guy at the third shop says. "It should take a couple hours for this shit to melt. The machine only died ten minutes ago, and this crap just started melting like Satan's cooling his nuts. Ghostbuster shit. I'm too scared to open the damn fridge."

As if that isn't bad enough, I trip over my own loose shoelace and nearly face-plant, but Rex is quick enough to catch me. I look up at him and say, "Mercury really is in the marmalade."

Sitting on a bench, staring out at the dark sea, I look up and find the constellation in the shape of a lightning bolt. I turn to ask Rex which one it is, but he's wearing an expression caught between sadness and confusion. "Sterling for your thoughts?" I ask.

He leans forward, hiding his face in his hands, his voice muffled, "I've taken you on the worst date ever."

"Well, that's technically not true," I say. "At least we made it to the top of the rainbow Ferris wheel before lightning struck that transformer."

He stares at me, unamused. "I wanted our evening to be romantic."

"We did get rescued by seven hunky firemen. Roberto even tried giving me his number."

He growls.

I nudge him playfully. "It was romantic being trapped way up high in the dark with you. The kiss made up for everything. If the sides hadn't been glass and cell phones didn't exist, we might've been able to do a little something-something else in the dark. Hey! We could lay in the bed of your truck and do that little something-something else."

He shakes his head. "With the way things have been going tonight, someone would rear-end us at top speed."

I shrug my shoulders. "Getting rear-ended wouldn't be the worst way I've spent a Saturday night."

He snorts. "What Saturday night could be worse than this one?" he asks, his voice laced with curiosity.

I smile, but it feels bittersweet. "Before you, I spent many Saturday nights alone and misunderstood."

His expression immediately softens, and he wraps an arm around me, as if trying to offer comfort. We sit in silence for a few moments. Then he asks, "Does the kiss really make up for all these mishaps?"

My heart aches with something I can't quite name, but it also feels like it can begin glowing. "Kiss me again, and it'll be the only thing I remember."

He leans in, his breath warm against my cheek, and when his lips meet mine, the world drops away until there's only the steady thrum of his heartbeat and the taste of him, like spun sugar melting on my lips. Vanilla and strawberries. Softy, airy, and impossibly sweet. He pulls back just enough to look at me, his thumb brushing my jaw, eyes searching mine. In answer to his unspoken question, I grip the front of his shirt to keep him close, and he kisses me again. Playful, sticky, and tender.

Chapter Eight

NOVEMBER 2025

A haunting recording of Wendy Rule keens in the background. Her voice is rich and spellbinding, like velvet draped in shadow. An ancient, witchy resonance, as if she's singing from the edge of the veil between earth and ether.

Large black obsidian towers surround the clamshell firepit on four sides. Alexandra explains they are powerful energy releasers and clearers, capable of absorbing and transmuting any negative emotions or thoughts. Their presence allows one to move forward with a lighter heart.

If I touch them, I wonder if they'll glow red hot and crack?

A multitude of crystals, amethyst for purification, and citrine for comfort, hang like delicate ornaments from two olive trees in large ceramic pots on either side. Alexandra looks as if she's standing between two pillars, and it reminds me of The High Priestess tarot card.

She tells me the three of us will wait to read our letters at the end, with me reading mine last.

This only brings my anxiety closer to the surface.

One by one, each guest steps forward and reads their letters of memories and farewells to Rex.

After finishing, they drop their letters into the bright flame to burn under the dark moon.

To them, each letter that goes up in flame is a symbol for release, a tiny fragment of Rex's soul set free into the universe, where it will one day become whole again and ready for reincarnation.

My stepmother's and father's letters genuinely surprise me.

They are being so kind and supportive.

They shine a loving light on our relationship.

I honestly hadn't known they'd been this observant.

They're celebrating what was and what could have been.

I feel the weight of everyone's eyes, and I struggle to keep my bottom lip from trembling.

I keep my gaze fixed ahead, focusing on the images on the screen as Clive reads his farewell letter to his son.

Halfway through, his voice falters, and tears overcome him. His only child is dead, and Alexandra cannot carry another.

Rex had told me she had to have a hysterectomy not long after giving birth to him.

I can't get over how nobody is angry. How come nobody is screaming? All these people in attendance and not a one is ranting about how crazy this is.

Warmth and kindness fill so many letters, but the spirit of wrath has written mine.

Rex killed himself, and nobody knows why.

No letter.

He'd carried me down a fucking mountain to some stranger's house and then preceded to blow out his brains beside my dying body.

My left eye twitches as Alexandra reads her farewell letter. It sounds like a script written for her to recite. These are not the words of a mother whose son has committed suicide.

Where are the questions?

Where is the outrage?

What made him do it?

How much pain was he in?

No.

Her letter contains nothing but acceptance and woo-woo "love and light" nonsense.

I know four months have passed, but my grief remains as raw as if the surgeon tore open my chest and ripped my heart out yesterday.

"I love you and I release you," she says, dropping her letter into the flame.

She stands there watching it burn as I watch the smoke rise upwards.

She then turns and makes room for me to step forward.

My nerves are exposed and aggravated.

I step forward and don't even open my letter.

I stare straight ahead at the images of Rex flashing on the screen. Swimming, swinging a bat, running in a race, shuffling cards.

I miss the sound of his shuffling. The riffle, the flick, the pop.

"I wanted to kill myself."

A few small gasps fill the silence as a breeze ruffles my hair. Faces in the crowd immediately look upset and concerned. I don't look at my parents.

"I came very close once..."

Small beads of sweat drip down my cheek.

"I still think about doing it, but I can't bear the thought of hurting something that doesn't belong to me. This heart isn't mine."

I keep staring at his happy face.

"I don't know what to do with this anger."

Lightning flashes overhead.

I close my eyes and whisper. "I miss you so much."

Thunder growls low, almost deadly.

"I've been told what this ceremony is about and it's bullshit. There is no releasing for me. There is no saying goodbye. Why didn't I see your pain? Why didn't I feel it? Is that why we were there? Were we trying to... I can't remember. Why can't I remember?"

I shake my head, trying to make everything fall back into place.

A vital spark of myself is missing.

Removing my heart took more than just a dying organ.

It stole a piece of me I'll never get back.

I'm not me anymore.

I lift my gaze back to the screen.

It flickers for but a fraction of a second and I see myself lying in the wet grass, with Rex kneeling over me.

"What the fuck is this?"

He's crying and mouthing something I can't hear.

"What's he saying?"

Seeing he's about to be tackled by two people wearing gold masks, he puts a gun to his head and pulls the trigger.

I scream, stumbling back a step.

My falling letter flutters unnoticed into the greedy flames as I watch him fall over beside me and kick.

"What the fuck?" I cry, pointing. "Who filmed that? Why would you show this?"

Heads turn towards the screen behind and then back at me with smiles on their faces. They look distorted and deranged.

"Why the fuck are you smiling?" I yell.

Why the fuck are they showing security footage?

He shoots himself, over and over, like a broken record stuck on repeat. A revenant trapped in perpetual torment.

"Turn it off!" I scream, rushing forward. "Turn it off! Turn it off! TURN IT THE FUCK OFF!"

I snatch up a chair, my vision blurring with rage, ready to hurl it—anything to release the pressure building in my chest and to stop that ghost in the machine.

The wind picks up.

"I'll wipe the smiles off your fucking faces!"

Thunder booms.

My dad surges forward, shouting my name, his body crashes into mine as he grapples for the chair. His hands fight mine, shaking with desperation.

Then—another set of hands grabs my arms from behind, dragging me back, and suddenly it's all noise and heat and panic.

Someone grabs me by the hair and sharply pulls my head back.

A ship takes shape—an old one, worn and weather-beaten, its sails torn by heartache and despair. Fog curls around its rigging like dragon smoke. He's there. Rex. Standing at the helm.

The sea churns violently around him, waves slamming against the hull. Then the water parts with an unnatural force. A massive hand—beautiful, shining, and terrifying—rises from the depths, dripping in jewels that burn.

Rex looks up, eyes wide.

The hand crashes down with terrifying speed.

"REX!" I scream.

"There is nothing there, sweetheart," Yvonne says, doing her best to calm me.

I'm back in the wet grass. There's so much blood—everywhere, all over me. Who are these two in their gold masks? They're each giving us CPR.

"Is this how it happened? Is this how he died?" I choke out, my body trembling. "MAKE IT STOP!"

"Make what stop?" my dad asks.

My parents and the Duttons buzz around me, their voices frantic as they try to soothe me, but I can't tear my eyes away from the horror on the screen.

Broken wood. Rex struggling in the water.

The lights shatter into frantic flickers—and there he stands, impossibly close.

Eyes glowing gold amidst the concerned crowd. Mouth open in a scream.

No.

I'm the one screaming.

"He's right there!" I yell, jabbing a trembling finger. "HE'S RIGHT THERE!"

He glides closer, his hand reaching out, as if to touch me.

The wind becomes a roar.

I struggle to break free, but a sudden, sharp sting pierces my skin.

I glance down and find I've been stuck with a needle—by my father.

"What the fuck?"

The wind dies.

My vision blurs and the world around me dissolves into a haze of distorted voices, each word disintegrating into unintelligible static.

Slowly, Rex's face swims into focus, his lips hovering just a breath away, an icy whisper brushing my ear like a wet tongue.

"Here I am."

Chapter Nine

June 21, 2025

"You live here?" I ask, trying my best to sound casual, though my voice betrays me as I nervously adjust my Barbie pink sunglasses. The house is a gleaming image worthy of a magazine's glossy cover.

"Technically, my parents live here," Rex replies, a smirk tugging at the corner of his mouth as he parks the car. "I occasionally get busted for robbing their fridge."

His parents greet us at the front door with the warmth that immediately makes me feel like this is a home.

Mrs Dutton, in her flowy pink and gold kaftan and effortless charm, kisses both my cheeks before asking if I'd like a freshly made lavender lemonade, while Mr Dutton, wearing an apron that reads MEAT DADDY, pulls me into a bear hug like I've always been part of the family.

"Really?" Rex asks, pointing at it. "Mom?"

She chuckles. "It is the tamest."

Mr Dutton nods. "My other says, 'Spit Happens' and 'I Flip, You Moan'."

Rex makes a face, and I laugh.

We spend the afternoon laughing, eating grilled seafood, and chatting by the pool. They want me to feel like family—I can tell. They're always checking if I need anything, but never overbearing.

I watch Mr Dutton man the grill with a comical level of focus, flipping prawns and steaks as if his brain's on a timer, while Mrs Dutton shares embarrassing stories about Rex's childhood.

Rex is taking it with surprising grace. Sharing anything from my childhood would mortify me.

"I wish you could have seen him at his seventh birthday party." Mrs Dutton laughs. "He wore this silly little blue cape and declared himself king of the jumping castle."

"Mom!" Rex exclaims, his cheeks flushing strawberry wine. "Any story but this one!"

Oh, so now we have a no-go topic. Tell me more! Spill the tea.

"What?" I ask, leaning forward, curious.

Now he's getting flustered. "No." Rex shakes his head firmly. "Don't you dare."

"What?" I repeat, turning to her for answers.

"He thought he was Superman." Mrs Dutton grins.

Mr Dutton walks over and hands me a prawn. "Let's just say that was my fault."

I take a bite. Perfectly seasoned.

"Both of you, be quiet," Rex commands, his voice a mock growl.

Mr Dutton shakes his head as he makes his way inside.

"No." I chuckle. "Tell me."

Mrs Dutton smirks. "He jumped right as Clive jumped, and Clive's weight sent him soaring. He looked like a little bluebird shooting through the air. I can laugh about it now."

And she does.

"I broke my wrist," Rex mutters, leaning back and crossing his leg with exaggerated nonchalance. "Other than that, it's still in my top three best birthdays."

"What makes number one?" I ask.

Mrs Dutton's expression turns instantly mischievous. She claps her hands. "Happy birthday to you, happy birthday to you…"

The glass door slides open, and my eyes widen as Mr Dutton appears with a chocolate cake in hand.

Rex reaches over, his fingers clasping mine. "Getting to spend this one with someone special."

I blink, surprised. "I did not know today was your birthday. Why didn't you tell me? I would've gotten you something."

"And miss that look of surprise on your pretty face?" Mrs Dutton interjects with a playful shake of her head. "Oh, no. Now that's a gift."

"Make a wish, son," Mr Dutton says, setting the cake down on the table.

A number 20 candle burns brightly at the centre of his cake.

Do you think I'm a demonic trash piece?

Ah! Of course! He's a Gemini. I feel like such an oblivious idiot.

Rex winks at me. He closes his eyes, his expression softening as if holding onto a secret thought. After a few seconds, he opens them again and leans forward, blowing out the flame.

After cake, we lounge by the pool, the sun warm on our skin and the water a stunning Greek blue. Rex pulls me in after I hesitate too long at the edge, and we end up splashing around, laughing until our stomachs hurt.

Today has been one of those moments in time that feels too perfect to truly be real, and yet here I am, walking as if through a dreamscape.

After Mom died, I didn't think I'd ever feel happiness like this again.

With the day coming to a close, his parents bid us goodnight, and Rex leads me up a flight of stairs to his bedroom.

It's bigger than the entire upstairs of my parent's house.

His bed looks as though it could fit an occult orgy, and floor-to-ceiling windows offering a breathtaking view of the night beyond their panes.

He takes a seat on the edge of his bed, towel-drying his wet hair, when he glances at me. "You have fun today?"

I nod, my mind still buzzing. "It's your birthday. Did you?"

"Yes. I did."

"You have amazing parents."

He smiles. "They're on their best behaviour. Trust me, they have their moments."

"Don't all parents?" I laugh. "Honestly, I'm surprised mine haven't killed me yet—with this venomous mouth and toxic attitude, I'm lucky they haven't cut my poisonous tongue out."

He places his towel aside, his expression shifting to something unexpectedly serious. "I wanted you to meet them because... well, because you're important to me. You're the first boy I've ever felt comfortable bringing home."

His words hit me like a golden arrow to the heart, and I don't quite know what to say, and I don't want to ruin this special moment building between us by saying something stupid.

He stands and walks over to me; his expression is unwavering. "Julian, I want you to be my boyfriend. Officially."

I remember him placing the Two of Cups on top of The Lovers. The ultimate soulmate card.

"When did you decide to pursue me?" I ask.

"The day we met, when I pulled the Two of Cups," he says. "I'd never done that before."

My reading has come true.

My heart does a little flip in my chest, and for a second time, angel wings carry away my ability to speak.

The sincerity in his voice, the way he is staring at me—it's impossible to ignore my feelings.

"You already grabbed me by the hair and dragged me to your parent's cave," I say, making him grin from ear to ear. "This is boyfriend territory, isn't it?"

I see his broad shoulders relaxing. "So, is that a yes?"

I clasp my hands behind my back, scuffing the ground with my toe as I struggle not to blush. "Yeah. I'll be your boyfriend, Rex Dutton."

Before I can say anything else, he pulls me into a tight hug.

I wrap my arms around him and we stay like this for a few heartbeats, neither of us in a hurry to let the other go.

When he releases me, I point to the dresser crammed with trophies. "Alright, I'm going to need an explanation for all that."

He groans. "Do I have to? It feels like a lifetime ago."

I chuckle, shaking my head. "No, you don't."

"Do you think your parents will let you come to my birthday party at Aetherlys tomorrow night?"

I shrug. "I don't see why not."

"I just figured... since you start school tomorrow..."

"My classes are online. I can always make up the hours over the weekend. Besides, you can hang out on my bed and be my guinea pig."

He raises an eyebrow, smirking. "I don't mind being a future massage therapist's guinea pig. Hey! I bet my parents will even let you do your internship with us."

I bite my bottom lip, hesitating. "My stepmom's set on me finishing my internship at her new spa."

"What's it called again?" he asks.

"Soluna," I reply.

He nods knowingly. "The sun and the moon."

"She's obsessed with this goddess. I think her name is Valorea or that might just be an epitaph. She's decorated the waiting area with bronze statues and large pieces of rose quartz and clam shells. Behind the service desk, there's this stunning pair of bronze wings mounted on the wall, so when you walk in, it looks like the staff are angels welcoming you. It's her way of promoting beauty and expressing love through self-care. You know, making sure your own cup is full before you serve others. Even though she's not my birthmother, I love her, and I want to support her, because she's always been there for me."

"And this," he says, taking my hands and guiding me toward his bed, "is exactly why I like you. Beneath all these snarky, wretched vibes you pretend to exude with such steely confidence, you're a glowing pool—warm, inviting, and impossible not to dive heart first into."

"How did you learn to speak like that?" I ask, allowing him to pull me onto the bed, settling with my head resting on his bare chest. "All those classes at the retreat?"

"I read a lot of books," he answers, wrapping his arms around me. "And I'm a romantic."

"I wish I could stay the night," I whisper.

His hands roam up and down my back.

I lift my head, and we kiss.

My hand slowly travels south, and I gently nip his bottom lip.

Gripping his hard length in my hand, I whisper, "Happy birthday, Rex."

Moving lower, I take him in my mouth.

He moans.

Thunder cracks and all the lights go out.

Chapter Ten

Apparently, I had a nervous breakdown and instead of admitting me to the Ministry of Mental Maintenance, my parents decided it was safer to keep me closer to home. Since Alexandra's a licensed counsellor and the retreat has round-the-clock staff, the Duttons agreed to let me lodge at Aetherlys.

Three weeks of yoga, guided meditations, smoothies, vegetarian meals, reiki, and talking about my feelings. They even ask me to keep a journal, but I don't write anything. Instead, I whisper my rage to a page, then I tear it out and rip it to shreds.

Alexandra stands beside me on the wooden bridge, dressed in white, her hand gently resting on my wrist. Aquamarine and Larimar rings glint on each finger, catching the light. "You know you can always share with me, Julian. This is the ultimate safe space."

My head still feels foggy from all the medication and vitamin infusions. "I can't remember what happened," I tell her, lifting my gaze and looking at her. "What did I do?"

She meets my stare with such grace and compassion, her eyes soft. "You've undergone tremendous change and suffered a substantial loss. A heart attack. Losing your... boyfriend. Discovering the choice your parents had to make to save your life. Four months of physical therapy. It's a lot for someone your age to be confronted with all at once."

A moment of silence.

"We should have known better and for that, I'm sorry. Of course, that ceremony would have been overwhelming for you. We... we didn't want you to feel excluded from something so precious. Rex loved you and we want you to feel a part of this family. Just know your parents love you and they couldn't bear the thought of losing you. They did what they felt was right in a moment of fear and panic. They chose you."

She's right. My parents faced an impossible choice—the only choice they could make when confronted with something so insane: take this stranger's heart, or lose your son.

Tick-tock. Tick-tock. Tick-tock.

I look down at the glittering water below and shut my eyes against the harsh glare. I've still not visited him. Seeing Rex's grave would seal the inevitability that he's truly gone and I will never see him again. I open my eyes and find many looking back. All the fish are staring up at me, their mouths gaping as if they want to spill the seaweed tea.

"They think you're going to feed them." She entwines her fingers with mine, giving my hand a squeeze. "Let's go see Maggie. She's got a relaxing session planned for you, and afterward, you can unwind in the float tank."

A breeze ruffles my shaggy hair as I follow her, my eyes lifting to the sky.

Dark clouds are moving in, preparing for another evening of rain that brings thunder to echo in my soul.

"Do you think I can visit Rex tomorrow?" I ask quietly.

She turns around with unshed tears in her eyes. "I thought you'd never ask."

I smile, and she draws me into a hug.

Maggie has a chunky piece of moldavite hanging around her neck. It's a translucent green with an etched surface. The chain it's on has it dangling near her heart.

Many believe moldavite to be a powerful transformation stone that speeds spiritual growth, enhances intuition, and facilitates deep emotional healing and cosmic connection.

I'd seen TikTok videos of young people who have worn moldavite and it had set their lives on fire... and not in the good way.

Unbalanced and ignorant new agers shouldn't treat something speeding through the cosmos and crashing into an adolescent society as a fashion accessory. If one's intentions were not clear, moldavite would make it transparent. Ancient people worshipped these pieces of celestial matter for a damn good reason.

"Here you are," she says.

She serves me a cup of blue lotus tea, infused with honey and saffron. She asks how I'm feeling and if I have any intentions I'd like to set before our session begins.

"Where are you from?" I ask.

"Germany." She smiles.

I nod and gaze down at the cup between my palms.

This new heart beats so strongly within me, keeping me alive—but is this what being alive is going to feel like from now on?

I spend time in the retreat's library, reading about ancient Egyptian views of the soul, and find myself fascinated by their perspective on the connection between the body, the heart, and the afterlife.

They believe an important part of the soul lives in the heart, which they consider the key to the afterlife. They see the heart as holding a person's essence, consciousness, and moral integrity—it isn't simply a physical organ.

I don't know how to fully explain it—because the heart, in their belief system, is far more than just a pump for blood. It is the seat of everything that makes a person human. And now, with this heart inside me, I can't help but wonder—have I lost a piece of my soul with it?

Am I still whole, or am I just a shadow of the person I once was, a changeling walking around with someone else's heartbeat in my chest? Has my separation from my heart locked it away somewhere beyond reach? And because this stranger's heart now lives inside me, is this keeping them from finding peace in the afterlife?

I finish the last sip of tea as she turns on soft whale songs that drift through the room on a stranger tide. From a neatly arranged tray, she chooses several small bottles of oils, explaining that each is infused with unique vibrations to support my intentions. Her calm, reassuring voice makes it easy to believe, even though I'm not sure I fully understood it.

"I'd really like to see you once a week. It'll give you something relaxing to look forward to—a little space just for you. Even if you don't believe in any of this, it believes in you, Julian. Ja?"

She asks me to remove my shirt. My skin prickles with unease as vulnerability creeps in.

Reluctantly, I comply, holding my arms across my chest, instinctively shielding the massive scar branding me.

Warm hands rest on my shoulders from behind, steady and reassuring.

"Never feel ashamed of such beauty," she says, her voice tender. "Wear your scar as if it's the most precious piece of jewellery in the world, because the true gem shines just beyond it."

She refers to my new heart as a gem, precious beyond compare. A gift of continuing life.

Taking my hand, she guides me over to the bed and instructs me to lie down on my back. "Relax," she whispers, her voice soothing as a lullaby. "I'm going to take you on a guided journey to help you find yourself again. Think of it as a sort of soul retrieval. Many cultures practice this... some are far more ancient than others."

"You're going to bring back a piece of my missing soul?"

"Ja. You will feel better afterwards."

The quiet flick of a lighter breaks the stillness, and moments later, the air fills with the sweetness of sandalwood and rose. Beneath its heady aroma, a deeper, shadowy note lingers—subtle, yet mysterious.

"I'm going to drip oils from above, so they pass through your aura."

Several warm drops land on my brow, and I feel her fingertips massage them in gentle, clockwise circles.

"This is Emerge and Glorify. We want your third-eye chakra shining like a brilliant crystal."

I draw in a deep breath. The scent is intoxicating.

Next, drops fall onto my chest.

Her hands follow, moving with the same deliberate care. "This is One Heart, Blossom, and Bliss. Your heart chakra will heal, and it will open like a beautiful lotus."

I breathe in again, feeling the oil's calming presence settle over me. No wonder Rex had loved these treatments. He always came out of them smelling like Easter morning—jellybeans and chocolate wrapped in neon cellophane grass and sunlight.

A few more drops touch my throat.

"One Voice will help you speak your truth without fear."

Then, droplets land on each wrist, and I catch the faint melody of her voice as she speaks something in what must be her mother tongue. I can't quite make it out, but I think I hear words about hands and crafting something new.

"True Purpose," she explains.

Finally, a few drops fall into my hair, and she massages them into my scalp, her fingers moving with rhythmic care.

"Rebirth," she hums, the word reverberating like a prayer. As her hands slide over my scalp, her voice softens into a reverent murmur. "Awake and bloom, divine spirit, magnify your light within this vessel. With one purpose, one voice, one heart, guide this transformation to wholeness and grace."

I want to ask her what she means by that, but my body feels too relaxed to respond. Even my eyelids feel impossibly heavy, sealed shut by the weight of whatever spell she's casting. All I can feel are her hands, warm and gentle, massaging my scalp, her fingers threading softly through my hair.

The rhythmic cadence of her prayer washes over me, repeating like a sacred mantra that sinks into my bones with the consistency of warm honey. The spaces within my marrow filling with something I can't explain, and I want to smile and revel in it.

Gradually, an even stranger sensation takes hold.

I feel as though I'm spiralling through an endless expanse of space, turning and turning, each rotation lifting me higher and higher.

Prismatic lights surround me, shifting and blending into an infinite spectrum of colours, enveloping me in their brilliance as I ascend further into unknown levels of something vast and unknowable.

And then there's darkness—not the kind that creeps in with the night or the shadow of a monster's hand that emerges from beneath a bed.

No, this is something else entirely.

This darkness is the sacred veil of creation itself, the womb of endless potential where life begins and the divine breathes life into the void.

I blink and stare into a pair of brilliant golden eyes, their radiant glow searing through the abyss.

A haunting litany echoes through the deep, the relentless crash of invisible currents against jagged undersea mountains.

All around me, jellyfish pulse with a bioluminescent glow, their translucent forms illuminating the dark like drifting stars.

From out of undulating obsidian ink, a luminous hand reaches beneath my flesh, passing effortlessly through muscle and bone, and closing around my heart.

Each squeeze ignites lightning through my arteries, which radiates thunder through my veins.

A voice speaks.

Soft, cold, inescapable.

The hush of coral reefs, the screams of gulls, the groan of shipwrecks.

"Here I am."

The vibration rolls over me like a storm buried in fathoms.

Each word laced with salt and thunder.

The sharp snap of fingers jolts me awake.

My gaze fixes on the skylight above, where heavy raindrops pound relentlessly.

When did it start raining?

How long have I been trudging through my subconscious?

"Welcome back to your body," Maggie's gentle voice comes from my right, drawing my attention as I turn my head to look at her, blinking a few times to adjust. "How are you feeling?"

"Okay," I reply, slowly sitting up and stretching.

That's when I realise something feels different—I don't feel tired or weighed down. I pause, searching for the right word.

"I feel... rested."

She nods, giving me a knowing smile. "Good. Take your time to orient yourself. I'll be back shortly with some tea. No rush."

She closes the door softly.

I slide off the table, grab my shirt from the chair, and slip it on. Running my fingers through my hair, I pause, catching the lingering scent of the oils on my hands. I can't help but bring them closer for another inhale—they smell so good.

I turn and stare at the painting on the wall at the head of the massage table.

A figure in the deep, reaching for the world above... or depending on perspective, perhaps she was reaching for a lost realm below.

A melodious tapping of knuckles sound at the door.

Maggie steps back inside, carrying a teacup in her hand.

She hands it to me and I take it from her.

"Thanks."

"You're welcome, dear."

The cup looks to be carved from the bluest larimar, the elegant handle mother-of-pearl topped with a pearl.

I lift the teacup to my nose, inhaling its soothing aroma. "What's in this one?" I ask.

She motions for me to join her as she sits down. "One of my favourites. It's a delicate blend of chamomile, lavender, lemon verbena, and a very special honey—ethically sourced, of course—from Nepal. The bees feed on a rare species of rhododendron, which gives it its unique flavour."

The tea is cold. "It's bittersweet," I note, the taste lingering on my tongue.

Maggie nods. "Just like life. A gentle reminder that every moment, no matter how bittersweet, is a treasure to cherish."

I take a few more sips, adjusting to the taste with each one, and place the cup down on the table between us.

"Have you ever used a float tank before?" she asks.

I shake my head. "I've heard of them, but never tried one."

"Think of it as a sensory deprivation tank," she explains. "It's an enclosed pod with water heated to match your body temperature. A high concentration of Epsom salts allows you to float effortlessly, promoting deep relaxation and mindfulness."

"Do I need to do anything before getting in?" I ask, taking another sip.

"Ja. There's a shower in the room to rinse off the oils from your skin," she informs me. "You can float nude or wear the swimsuit provided—it's entirely your choice. The pod lid can stay open or closed, depending on what makes you comfortable. Inside, there's a light you can adjust and an option to play music via Bluetooth. All you need to do is lie back, float, and relax. Just avoid touching your face—the saltwater will sting your eyes. A gentle chime will signal the end of the session. Afterward, you'll shower off the salt and enjoy a glass of goji berry juice with pomegranate and food-grade essential oils added. It is a cult... retreat favourite."

"Occult?" I ask.

She nods. "Ja! Think of it as a restorative potion for the soul."

I finish the last sip from the cup, which likely cost more than all my course textbooks combined. I give it back to her and follow her out of the treatment room.

Freshly showered and standing nude in the soft light, I steady my nerves and step into the float tank. The sharp scent of concentrated saltwater tickles my nose, and the warm, shallow pool within softly laps against my ankles. I lower myself into it, my body effortlessly rising to the surface. With a hesitant breath, I reach up and bring the pod lid down, which immediately envelopes me in a deep indigo glow. I recline, reach up and turn off the light, letting the darkness settle in. The only sounds filling the space are the steady rhythm of my breath and the lub-dub of the heart beating in my chest.

Well, this certainly feels strange. It's like I'm not even in water.

This is because the water matches my body temperature. I feel suspended in the air.

Bursts of light explode behind my eyelids, vibrant and unexpected, like I'm gazing into a kaleidoscope.

Faint music drifts from the distance. Soft, barely audible, but growing louder with each passing moment.

I open my eyes, and the light show doesn't stop. Bursts of pale blue, green, and ghostly silver flickers in the surrounding darkness that swirls.

My heart pounds in my chest, matching the beat of the music that's deafening me. It is 'Apocalypse' by Cigarettes After Sex.

The music presses in from all sides, filling every inch of the pod.

The indigo light above turns on and begins flickering. I shoot up, barely avoiding hitting my head against the roof of the pod.

Between my legs, a large hand breaks the surface, grabbing my inner thigh with a cold, unyielding grip.

I collapse backwards, splashing water into my eyes.

Pain and panic surge through me.

I scream as my eyes tear from the stinging. Thrashing violently, I kick my legs, desperate to be free from that death grip.

"WHAT THE FUCK DO YOU WANT?" I scream over the pounding music.

I squint through the stinging pain and see another hand emerge from the water.

Cold fingers latch onto my other thigh and dig in.

I scream again as his face breaks the surface as if he's crawling up from the depths of some deep blue abyss, climbing the length of my salt slick body.

Rex comes face-to-face with me, his eyes glowing gold orbs. His hand rests on my forehead.

I see his book on the floor of his bedroom. The key bounces. A number 7.

His lips hover near my left ear and he whispers, "Locker."

He brushes his thumb across my cheek, placing a kiss at the corner of my mouth. Before I can embrace him in return, I feel something large move beneath me, and something pulls him under.

I cry out, reaching out in desperation, but before I can dive after him, the pod's lid lifts, and blinding white light floods in.

"Julian?"

"Maggie!" I hiss through the burning sting.

"What happened?" Alexandra's voice follows, frantic. "Are you okay?"

"My eyes!"

"Here." Maggies places a bottle in my hand. "Distilled water."

I hold the bottle up and squeeze it, allowing the cool water to pour over my eyes, the gentle flow gradually easing the sting and providing me with some relief.

"What happened?" Alexandra repeats.

I suddenly freeze in embarrassment.

I'm naked.

I curl into myself, pulling my legs tightly against my scarred chest and wrapping my arms around them.

"What?" she asks, her hand gently resting on my slick shoulder.

"I don't know," I mutter, shaking my head. "Maybe a panic attack... or maybe I fell asleep and had a nightmare. I can't remember."

Of course, I'm lying.

It's Rex.

Rex is here.

He's haunting me. Because he killed himself, is he now doomed to walk the earth forever?

My heart beats like a drum in my chest.

I look up at them both, a sinking feeling in my gut.

Something is terribly wrong, and he's trying to tell me what it is.

The key. The number 7. Locker... It's a key to a locker!

"Come on," Maggie says gently, taking my arm. "Let's get you to your room." She helps me out of the pod, steady and patient, while Alexandra stands by with a bathrobe. "I'll bring you something light to eat," she adds, her voice soft with care.

There's that sweet smell again. Filling my senses and clouding my mind.

Chapter Eleven

I don't intend to make Rex late for his birthday party the next night, but it's unavoidable. I change outfits twelve times, and none of my shoes seem quite right.

Eventually, I settle on something light—a look straight out of Byron Bay. White cotton shorts, an apricot fringed cardigan, and black thongs. Flip-flops, not butt floss.

I add a touch of eye makeup and highlighter to elevate my look and study my reflection in the mirror. My face is all sharp angles and polished cheekbones, just the way I like it. Slipping on my oversize sunglasses, I head downstairs, where the birthday boy is waiting patiently for me.

He lies on the sofa, eyes closed, sleeping like Count Dracula.

"Come on, ya old cunt," I say, taking his arm and pulling on him. "Get your ass up. We have a birthday to celebrate."

"No," he whines. "I was asleep. What did you wake me up for?"

"Your one year closer to the grave celebration."

"Grr."

"Come on, ya demonic trash piece. Can't keep the garbage collectors waiting."

Rex rises with a cocky little smile. I start to turn away, but he gives my ass a playful slap and spins me back into his arms, kissing me slow and deep.

"Bitch," he teases, voice low against my glossed lips.

"Your bitch," I whisper, trying to pull away—half-heartedly.

He laughs, squeezing my ass with both hands, and kisses me again.

Night is falling when we arrive, and I'm so glad I have my sunglasses on. I don't want anyone to see how wide my eyes have gone.

I can't believe how many people have rocked up. Is it even possible for someone to know this many people?

Even though Rex approves of my outfit, I'm relieved to see that other guests have made the same dress choice as us. It makes me feel instantly better—like I belong.

Getting to the front steps feels like a Met Gala event. Rex can't take two steps without stopping to shake hands and introduce me. I smile politely, shake hands in return, and repeat the cycle.

There's no way I'll remember all these names and connections, but everyone seems genuinely thrilled to be here. He completely captivates them, and they want to monopolise as much of his attention as they can. I can't tell if it's endearing or just weird.

"Hello," I say, smiling as he introduces me to each person that stops us. "Hi. Lovely to meet you. So nice to see you again. I'll never remember your name if I cared too. Ah-ha ha! Oh, I love the face cream. I'll tell Yvonne hi for you. Do you think I need a haircut? My sunglasses? Oh, is that why it's so dark?"

He takes me by the arm, guiding me up the stone steps. At the top, we enter the open-air lobby, where a path of dry seagrass and flowers stretch before us. We follow its path up a winding staircase and into the restaurant.

Ambient hang drumming floats through the air. To me, hang drumming carries an Atlantean vibe—its resonant, metallic tones ripple like light through ancient water, echoing the forgotten hymns of a sunken civilisation. Each note feels like a whisper from a mystical coastal market, where exotic incense mingles with salt air and spiritual seekers trade in memory and dreams. An instrument that stirs the soul with the rhythm of a bygone world, half-dreamed, half-remembered.

Iridescent lighting bathes the space in shades of lavender, pale blue, and gold. Gauzy, shimmering drapes cascade from the ceiling like glittering trails of stardust, while above, a large circular skylight showcases a glowing 3D constellation spiralling in midair.

The star reminds me of the chaos and beauty of the sea amid a storm.

"The Tempest takes the shape of a great wave rising from the ocean, crowned with a jagged lightning bolt. Suspended above the sea, it is the only constellation that has a truly fixed location and is only visible in this hemisphere," Rex says.

"Fixed?" I ask.

He nods. "No matter what time, day or night, it never moves."

I marvel at it.

"People here are obsessed with it. Some whisper it is a prison."

"Tempest," I whisper in awe and then blink as his words register in my head. I turn to look at him. "Prison?"

"Yep. A clink in the sky. Chained in starry suspension as punishment for a capricious and mercurial nature."

"You make it sound like there's a monster up there."

He shrugs. "Could be. Who knows what's swimming between all those stars?"

"I love your brain."

"Oh?" He asks, winking. "Just my brain?"

I smirk. "And your dick. I really like your dick."

He grins. "My dick really likes you, too."

I laugh.

Beneath the twirling constellation stands a round table draped in a silken cloth, adorned with large pieces of pyrite in huge clam shells, flickering candles, a massive bouquet of proteas and gifts in all shapes and sizes, wrapped in the same prismatic paper.

"Wow," I say, slipping off my sunglasses. "I can only imagine what they'll do when you turn twenty-one."

I glance up at him, and for a moment, he just stands there, his gaze lingering on me.

"What?" I ask.

"You're beautiful."

I smile, feeling a warmth spread through me at his appreciation. "Thank you."

"There's the man of the hour," Mr Dutton announces as he strolls up beside us, Mrs Dutton on his arm. "We were thinking you'd skipped town."

"I'm so sorry," I apologise, holding up my hands. "It's entirely my fault—outfit malfunction."

Mrs Dutton's face lights up with a warm, approving smile. She is practically beaming at me. "Come," she says, taking my arm in her own. "Let us speak of many things."

I glance back at Rex, whose dad is now guiding him through a pair of double doors, labelled "Staff Only".

"Rex tells me you've begun school to get your diploma in massage therapy." She draws me back, steering me toward the drinks.

She picks up a tulip shaped glass full of sparkling punch and hands it to me. I take it with a quiet thanks and nod. "Yes, that's right. I want to help my stepmother with her spa."

"That's wonderful." She gently clinks her glass against mine. "Have you considered splitting your internship between two businesses?"

I blink, surprised.

"This way, you can experience both worlds," she explains. "A specialised boutique and a five-star spiritual retreat. Both would look stellar on your resume. You would get a job anywhere, but I doubt you will ever want to leave paradise."

I'm not sure how to respond, so I take a careful sip of my drink, making sure not to spill any of the red liquid on myself. That's always the risk when wearing anything lighter than the shade of sin. Wearing white dooms you to splash something on yourself.

"That's incredibly generous," I say. "I don't think my parents would have any objections. In fact, they'd probably be thrilled."

"It's settled then," she says, clinking her glass against mine once more. "Yay!"

I nod, feeling less anxious now.

She leads me to a chair with a place card bearing my name. "Make yourself comfortable. I'll check on the boys and we'll get started soon." I watch her walk away and disappear through the same doors. Leaning back in my chair, I pull out my phone and see a new text from Rex. It's a jumble of capital letters that made no sense.

> LSYEHATR

I check the timestamp—he'd sent it three minutes ago. I quickly reply.

> Are you having a seizure?

I wait a few moments, but there's no response. Must be a butt-text.

The background music skips, and I glance up at the flickering lights. Laughter from a nearby table shifts into angry shouting, followed by a sharp slap.

I turn just in time to see a glass shatter on the floor and two girls going at each other.

Sitting alone at a nearby table, an elderly woman cackles, her finger pointing at the unfolding chaos in glee. Sensing she's being looked at, she slowly turns her head and her eyes lock onto mine. She falls silent; her gaze is intense and unwavering. She frowns, her face morphing into a caricature of a human. It's unsettling, like she doesn't belong in her own skin. She has that uncanny valley vibe that makes me want to break a glass and dare her to come near me. She smiles again, displaying small, but very sharp, eel-like teeth.

I gasp as the lights turn off, and then back on.

The two girls are hugging each other, and the old woman is nowhere to be seen.

I scan the room, confused.

What the fuck was that?

Where the hell has she gone?

She was right there!

No way that old biddy can move that fast.

Just as I'm about to push my chair back and stand, the double doors swing open, and Rex enters the room with his parents on either side of him. Maggie and Suzannah follow behind.

He walks with an air, a presence I've never seen in him before. He stops near the gift table, positioned under the spiralling constellation. The light hits his brow, making his forehead appear oddly shiny.

I brush the feeling off, attributing it to the humidity—despite the fans twirling faster than Stevie Nicks.

But he's not looking at me. In fact, he's not looking at anything. He's just standing there, his gaze light years in the distance.

Nobody home.

He takes the microphone from his mother and smiles, but it isn't his smile. This smile belongs to someone else—a stranger I haven't met.

"I want to thank everyone for coming to my celebration," he says. Even his voice sounds unfamiliar—older, much deeper. "Dance, drink, eat, be merry."

The cerulean constellation above flashes and I can see golden rings and precious jewels being fed to the sea.

I blink as his captivated audience claps, and then his expression shifts. His eyes lock onto mine, and for a moment, I think I see a flicker of panic in them and he looks a little unbalanced on his feet. But just as quickly, he smiles—there it is, the face I know, but it looks forced... like he's putting on a show for everyone.

He sets the microphone down on the table, hugs his parents, and then walks straight toward me. Extending his hand, he pulls me to my feet, guiding me away from the table and the party.

Glancing over my shoulder, I notice Suzannah and Maggie deep in conversation with his parents, their expressions serious. "Where are we going?" I ask, confusion creeping into my voice.

"Away from here," he replies, leading me back downstairs and outside.

"Are you okay?" I ask, feeling concerned. "What happened?"

He doesn't answer. Instead, he opens the car door for me and motions for me to get inside, which I do. I watch him walk around the front of the car before sliding into the driver's seat.

"What is going on, Rex?" I ask again, my worry growing.

"I don't know," he says, turning the engine on. Then he looks at me, his eyes wild and unsettled. "But... I'm missing time... again."

"What?" I ask, fastening my seatbelt.

He bites his bottom lip, his fingers drumming anxiously against the steering wheel.

"I don't remember letting go of your hand. We walked in, met my parents... and then I was standing there with a microphone. It's happened before."

I stare at him, my mind racing. "Are you serious?"

"Of course, I'm serious!" he snaps, then immediately squeezes his eyes shut, as if trying to compose himself. "I'm sorry," he says, turning to me and reaching for my hands. "I'm sorry. I didn't mean to raise my voice at you like that. I'm just... I don't know where I went."

"If you're sure you don't want to stay here, let's go back to my house," I tell him, leaning forward and squeezing his hands, trying to ground him. "We can lock ourselves away in my bedroom and you can tell me everything... if you're comfortable doing so. Or we can just watch Netflix and chill."

He looks as if he's thinking it over for a moment, then nods. "If I can't share with you, who can I share with?"

I reach up and run the pad of my index finger over his shiny brow, then bring it to my nose. It smells like some kind of essential oil blend—floral mixed with citrus... and something darker... coppery. "Why do you have oil on your brow?" I ask him.

He shrugs, putting the car in reverse and backing up. "I don't know."

His cell phone rings, but he immediately silences it.

He's curled up beside me, nestled in my arms. 'Offering' by Black City Lights plays softly in the background as I run my fingers through his hair.

He opens up to me about the missing time, and the more he shares, the tighter the knot in my chest grows. He tells me it isn't the first time—it's been happening for weeks.

I ask him to elaborate.

One moment he's at Cairns Central, and the next, he's at Palm Cove with no memory of how he got there. He even wakes up in his car in the middle of the night, parked in the driveway, with more than half a tank of petrol gone—despite filling up that same morning. He doesn't remember leaving the house, let alone driving anywhere.

And now it happens right in front of me, and I don't even realise it. He can't remember letting go of my hand.

"You were not yourself. Your face was vacant, and your voice was unfamiliar, even your smile was twisted. You looked as though something—or someone—was possessing you, like another personality was overshadowing you. You in front of me now, this is the real you."

He hugs me tighter. "I feel like little pieces of me are being stolen."

I can feel his panic beginning to bleed over into me. "It's okay." I rub small, soothing circles across his back.

The candle on my bedside table flickers, casting shadows across the ceiling. I stare at them, feeling the warmth of his breath against my neck.

"Can I share something with you now?" I ask as he plants a kiss against my shoulder blade.

"Of course."

"When you were in the back room, something strange happened."

"What?"

"The music started skipping, and the lights flickered," I say, my pulse quickening at the memory. "Then, a fight broke out, and there was this old woman sitting by herself. She was laughing—this eerie, unsettling laugh—and when she turned to look at me..." I hesitate, searching for the right words. "She didn't look right. Her skin was too tight, like she was wearing something that didn't fit. It was... wrong."

"What happened?"

"The lights went out for a moment, then came back on, and the music returned to normal. The two girls who'd been fighting were hugging like nothing had happened between them, and the old woman was gone. It was like she'd never been there."

"You think you saw a ghost?"

"I don't know." I shrug. "Did I? Is the retreat haunted?"

"It shouldn't be. My parents blessed and made it sacred grounds."

"Then I don't know what it was," I tell him, turning around to meet his eyes. "But whatever it was... I know I experienced something."

"Perhaps we are both crazy and need to be admitted to the Department of Misaligned Realities." A wry smile playing on his lips.

I snort, shaking my head. "That's not funny."

"Then why'd you snort?" he teases.

"Because you're ridiculous."

"You're ridiculous. Ridiculously beautiful."

"Rex, I believe you. Something real is happening," my tone soft but firm. "That part is absolutely true. You don't need to joke it off with me."

"Thank you." He rests his head against my chest with a heavy sigh. "I'm going to be in so much trouble. Everyone went to so much effort and I just bailed."

"You can always apologise," I whisper, running my fingers through his hair again in soothing strokes. "Blame it on me—say my anxiety got the better of me, and you had to step in to protect everyone."

He laughs softly. "From you? A little dandelion?"

I chuckle, brushing a strand of his hair back. "I don't mind being the scapegoat this one time, if it keeps you out of trouble."

He hugs me tighter. "Your willingness to be my Jesus really touches me, but my conscience won't allow it. Besides, they'd never buy it. Even if you were anxious, you walked into that room on my arm like a prince."

"Oh, I was terrified. Large gatherings make me nervous as fuck. You're lucky I didn't run and hide in the bathroom or slide under the snack table."

We sit in silence for a few moments.

"I'd love to know how you got that oil on your brow," I finally say, breaking the stillness.

He frowns, his head tilting slightly. "It must've happened while I was in the back room."

"I'd like to get my hands on a bottle," I tell him, a note of curiosity creeping into my voice. "Just to see what's actually in it."

He glances up at me, a mischievous glint in his eyes. "I think I can manage that."

I grin, my smile widening at the thought.

"Maggie keeps a box of oils above the sink, only for my sessions," he continues, lowering his voice like it's a secret. "I think I can borrow one without her noticing."

I nod, a smirk playing at the corner of my mouth. "Cool."

He raises an eyebrow. "Who do you know?"

I lean in slightly, lowering my voice. "Well, I have this acquaintance who's into chemistry. She might help."

"Do you think I'm being hypnotised or mind-controlled?" he asks, his voice tinged with uncertainty. "Or maybe having hallucinations because there's some chemical in the oils?"

I pause for a moment, considering his question. "I don't know," I say. "But honestly, it makes more sense than ghosts or being taken over by some outside force. The oils could mess with your head, maybe in ways we don't even realise."

"Then that would mean my parents know about this," his voice dropping with a hint of realisation.

I shake my head. "Not necessarily. This could be the work of someone they trust—feeding them all this woo-woo, making them believe you're losing it, and getting your parents to rely solely on them to fix you."

"But how do you explain your experience tonight?" he asks. "Nobody else seemed to notice any of this."

I pause, thinking it over, and then my jaw drops. "Your mom gave me a glass of punch... but I can't remember if she ladled it or if it was already prepared. I was so nervous about being left alone with her. I wasn't really paying attention."

"I don't want to go home tonight," he whispers. "What if I black out again?"

I shake my head. "I'm shocked they didn't stop you driving."

"Also," he says, giving me another serious look. "I don't think it's all just in our heads. I've been doing my cards... and I keep getting the same three, no matter how many times I shuffle them."

What? No way! "Which three?" I ask.

"The Devil, The Tower, and Death," he answers.

I know just enough about tarot to understand those are terrible cards to draw.

"And when I drew a single card from the Deste, I got the same card every time. I even threw the deck onto the ground and that card was the only one turned over facing me."

"Which card was that?"

"Valinde."

"I know these cards are bad, but what do they mean regarding you?"

"The Devil represents chains that bind you, entrapment. The Tower is a breaking point, shocking and violent. There is no escape from the fall. The Death card is all about reckoning, changing, transformation, sacrifice, and possibly a literal death. With everything that is happening to me, the cards are basically telling me I am being bound by an outside force. The truth is coming, and the outcome will not be gentle. The life I know is going to be destroyed and I don't know if there will be anything to rebuild once whatever this storm is passes."

I shiver and ask, "And this Valinde card?"

"Valinde is the bringer of misfortune and doom. She is associated with secrets, curses, malice, black magic, and hidden dangers. Her presence is a warning to beware of deception and manipulation. A dark goddess. Some refer to her as the horrible old woman."

"A horrible old woman?" I ask, getting immediate goosebumps.

He nods, and then his eyes widen. "Oh... Oh crap."

I get up and walk over to my bookshelf and pick up my Pamela Coleman Smith deck I'd purchased from Happy Herbs and bring them over to him. "Show me."

He takes the deck from me and slides the cards out into his hands and begins shuffling them. Taking a deep breath, he draws three and hands them to me.

I flip the first one over and gasp.

The Devil.

I flip the second card over.

The Tower.

Hand shaking, I flip over the third card.

Death.

"No, no, no," I say, shaking my head, handing the cards back to him. "Do it again."

I watch him closely this time.

He spreads the deck out on the bed and tells me to pick them. I don't pick the top three or the bottom three. I pick three cards randomly from different spots.

It's the same three cards in the same order!

"This can't be real," I mumble, putting the cards back into the deck and I mess them up between us. "Now take them and throw them on the ground."

As he picks up the deck to do so, three cards slip out onto the bed. I watch him reach for them and turn them over.

The Devil, The Tower... and Death.

Immediately, every hair on the back of my neck rises.

A knock at my bedroom door makes me yelp, as if Death herself has come calling. We both turn as my stepmother walks in, carrying a tray with two glasses and two bowls of what smells like my dad's award-winning beef stew.

"Since you weren't at the party for long, I thought you boys might be hungry," she says, setting the tray down on my desk and turning to face us. "You two better not be opening any portals in here with those cards."

"Thanks," I smile, sitting up beside Rex. "And no. No portals. Hey, do you think Rex could crash on the couch? I'm not comfortable with him driving home so late."

She crosses her arms as she thinks about my request for a few seconds. "I don't see why not... if he stays on the couch. I'm too young to be a grandmother."

"Yvonne!" I shout, grabbing a pillow.

She dashes from my room, laughing as I chuck it after her.

"Oh, she thinks she's funny," I seethe.

But then the growl from Rex's stomach cuts through my embarrassment. I glance at him over the scary tarot cards.

"I don't understand," I say, gazing down at them. "How is this possible? I've asked the same question over and over before and I get different cards every time."

He shakes his head. "I don't know, but something is happening."

"Let's eat," I suggest. "Afterward, I'll burn some frankincense and I'll set you up on the couch."

He gets up and fetches the tray before I can.

"Have you shared any of this with your friends?"

He returns to the bed with the tray in hand, shaking his head as he sets it down between us before passing me a bowl. "Most of them are cum shots their mothers should have choked on."

My jaw drops.

"Stale as old toast and emotionally bankrupt."

"Stop!"

"So surface-level, they dive headfirst into the shallow end."

"Damn!"

"Puddles to be driven through."

"Hush!"

"Deep conversations trigger their thalassophobia."

"I take it you don't have any real friends then."

"I have friends." He puts a spoon full of stew into his mouth, and closes his eyes for half a second. I can tell he really likes it. There's a reason my dad always wins first prize. "But the moment you want to have a serious conversation about something that matters, their skin crawls and they quickly want to change the subject or flee to the nearest shop. Oh, but you better be there when they want to bitch about something or someone, otherwise you'll end up the topic of the night for being a narcissist."

I can't help but smile at him as he takes another bite.

"I have never cared what people think of me. In fact, I encourage the worst."

He chuckles. "I'll protect your image."

I grin. "I have SPF and sunglasses for that."

He laughs.

"With friends like this, how on earth did you keep who you really were a secret from me for two months?" I ask.

"Money," he answers honestly. "And secrets nobody wants dressed up real fancy and paraded down Macrossan in full daylight."

"You're serious?" I ask.

"Welcome to far superior Port Douglas." He shrugs. "The Golden Zone."

He's only repeating what I overhear at the Mossman Markets nearly every Saturday morning.

"I find it interesting."

"What?" he asks.

"When I mention Mossman, some people here get 'that' look on their faces."

He nods and put on a convincingly posh accent. "Oh, darling! We never go to Mossman on purpose. We only travel north to brunch in Cape Tribulation."

He has me laughing because it's a fantastic mimicry.

"Joking and local gossip aside," he says, putting his empty bowl down on the tray. "This has been a beautiful and friendly place to grow up in."

I agree. "Being gay, I actually feel safe walking around at night. I honestly never want to go back. I don't have to worry about pew-pews and unhinged wee-woos."

He reaches for my hand. "Good."

After smudging the cards and ourselves with frankincense, Dad lays down the law, making it crystal clear: if he even suspects anything under blanket, he'll be on the phone with Rex's parents to come pick him up.

Rex quickly promises, "Nothing under blanket will happen, sir."

I back him up. "I don't want him driving home this late. There are too many people in town who've been drinking."

Dad mutters under his breath, waving over his shoulder as he goes upstairs with Yvonne to their bedroom.

I set up the couch for him—spreading a sheet, fluffing a pillow, and handing him a light quilt. Before heading to my room, I kiss him on the cheek and say, "Try to get some rest. If you need anything, text me—I'll turn up the volume on my phone so I hear it. The last thing I need is Dad catching you in my room after making a promise."

"Thank you," he says, pulling me into a hug so tight he lifts me right off my feet. "Have a good night," he adds as he sets me back down.

"You too," I reply, watching him settle on the couch before heading to my room.

I'm not sure how long I've been asleep when a deafening clap of thunder jolts me awake.

Sitting upright in bed, my heart races as flashes of lightning light up the room in quick succession.

Rex stands at the foot of my bed.

In the strobing flashes of lightning, I noticed he's shirtless. My eyes lock onto the left side of his chest, and my throat tightens as I swallow hard.

Beneath his skin, his heart glows—pulsing a gentle golden radiance.

I blink, and the glow vanishes.

He'd just woken me.

I must be seeing things.

"Rex!" I hiss under my breath, reaching over and turning my lamp on. "What are you doing?"

He stands there, eyes half-open, distant and unseeing. Is he sleepwalking?

Carefully, I rise from my bed and circle around to him, gently taking his arm. I know better than to wake him. How had he made it up the stairs without tripping and breaking his neck?

I notice he's holding something in his left hand. I carefully take it from him and find it to be a tarot card.

The Queen of Cups reversed.

Unpredictable.

Destructive.

Calm one moment, raging the next.

People pulled into emotional and literal depths.

I don't trust myself to get him back downstairs without risking a fall. He's bigger than me, and one wrong step could take us both out. The Tower and Death indeed. I put the card down and take him by the hand. It will be safer to let him take my bed while I go downstairs to sleep on the couch.

I carefully guide and ease him down onto the mattress. In the intermittent flashes of lightning, his half-open eyes seem to follow me, but I know he wasn't really seeing me. Gently, I brush my fingers through his hair a few times before pulling the sheet up around him, snugly tucking him in. I lean down, and kiss his brow before quietly making my way downstairs... only to almost slip on something and break my neck.

Muddy footprints on the tiles.

I gasp.

The front door's wide open.

Has he been outside?

Heart pounding, I rush over and stand in the open doorway, the stormy breeze ruffling my hair. I step back, close the door, locking the deadbolt with a sharp click.

Turning around, I pull out my cell phone and switch on my flashlight. The beam illuminates a trail of muddy footprints leading from the front door to the stairs and up.

I follow the trail as quietly as possible, each creak of the floorboard amplifying my unease.

How had I not slipped and killed myself?

The footsteps lead straight to my room.

Quietly, I step inside and see him lying there, his eyes now closed, his breathing soft and steady.

Being careful not to wake him, I carefully lift the edge of the sheet and shine the light at his feet.

Drying mud cakes them.

I exhale slowly, my chest tightening with concern. Leaving him alone no longer feels like an option. Whatever is happening—whether it's some drug-induced hypnosis or unexplainable supernatural woo-woo bullshit—one thing is clear: Rex needs someone to keep him safe.

Chapter Twelve

DECEMBER 2025

Dark clouds churn over the cemetery, pregnant with the weight of the impending deluge. Thunder rumbles as Alexandra and I get out of her car.

She walks ahead, guiding me towards the gates, but pauses at the threshold. Turning, she gestures towards the path that will lead me to my destination. Without a word, it's clear—she wants to give me privacy to be alone.

Wind whispers off the rows of weathered tombstones, smelling faintly of cut grass and damp earth as my footsteps crunch softly against the gravel path. I slowly approach Rex's grave for the first time, the bouquet of sunflowers trembling slightly in my hands.

So much time has passed that the grass has already grown around his headstone. An amethyst and a moonstone rest on top.

I kneel and place the flowers at the base, smoothing the ribbon tied around the stems.

Adoration.

That's what sunflowers mean.

It feels as if I'm reaching out to penetrate the veil of separation as I touch his headstone.

I crouch there and stare at the etched letters of his name—REX DUTTON.

That night is fragments glittering in the dark echo of my fucked-up recollection.

My mind is a broken mirror, shards of memory scattered across a dark room, reflecting distortions that make no sense.

What made us to go to Cooktown?

There's no way my dad would ever grant me permission to take such a long trip with my boyfriend—especially an overnight trip.

Even though I'm eighteen and legally considered an adult now—I live under my dad's roof—and modern Americans do not differ from their repressed pilgrim ancestors.

Sex is dirty. Sex is a sin.

Yet sex is everywhere we look.

Television. Magazines. Video games. Movies. Internet. Nature.

Did Rex and I elope?

Is that why his ring is on my thumb?

I tilt my head, straining to break through the dense fog clouding my thoughts. The harder I try pushing forward, the thicker it grows—like a heavy, viscous goo clinging to me, sucking at my feet, slowing every step as if determined to keep me from moving any closer to the truth I seek.

A drop of rain lands on my hand, distracting me.

Another droplet.

Water...

The float tank.

Another drop.

I'd been in the float tank last night.

Saltwater burning my eyes.

A hand.

A hand reaching out of the water and grabbing me.

Another drop.

I gasp.

Rex!

I hear the thud of a fallen book. The noise a bouncing key makes on tile. A number seven burned into my mind like a brand.

My memory. How had I forgotten?

Something or someone was screwing with my memories.

Maggie? Alexandra?

Oils.

Maggie had rubbed oils on my brow and temples before I went to sleep last night... and had been whispering words I couldn't understand.

I clench my jaw, my fingers brushing over the cool granite. If I can just push through this fucking fog, I might see something.

Wind whips through the cemetery, making the flowers quiver where they lie. I look up and scan the horizon, exhaling slowly as another few drips of rain land on my cheeks.

His naked body entwined with mine, gripping my arms, eyes burning with a gold fire, frigid breath in my ear.

"Locker."

7 is a locker! That's what the key is for. That's what he wants me to find. My answers would be in locker 7.

Escape.

I need to get away.

Thunder rumbles, rolling closer now. Wind rustles the trees. A curlew screams.

I tighten my grip on the headstone and rise, brushing cut grass from my knees. I glance down one last time at the sunflowers—the bright yellow petals like tiny golden bursts of sunlight against the shadows stone.

I run my palm across his name.

"I love you."

A whole multitude of banshees scream, and I take off running.

I LOVE YOU.

Chapter Thirteen

June 2025

Getting our hands on a bottle of Maggie's oils had been surprisingly easy—almost disappointingly so. I braced myself for a full-on covert operation. I was dressed all in black and had my big-ass Kim Kardashian sunglasses on. Hell, I was even wearing my 'rob the blue diamond from around your dead ex-husband's little whore's throat while she's sleeping' type shoes on.

We needlessly crept through shadows, ducked behind conveniently placed potted plants, and traded frantic, obscene hand signals just for shits. I even had our entire getaway planned as if we were Edina and Patsy trying to escape from attending Saffy's release from prison.

But no. None of that.

The heist is quick. Casual. More boring than listening to a Sunday sermon.

While I kept lookout, Rex strolled into the treatment room like his parents owned it, opened the cabinet, pulled out the wooden box, and plucked a bottle as if he were grabbing a glazed strawberry off an ex's wedding cake.

I even tried bribing a nine-year-old to at least raise the alarm, but the little cross-eyed crotch goblin called me a TEMU Jeffrey Starr and told me to get fucked. Rex had to hold me back from picking up the broken condom and punting the little mistake across the yard.

Now I'm sitting in the passenger seat while Rex zooms down Port Douglas Road.

I hold the tiny 7ml bottle in my hand, my eyes lingering on the handwritten label neatly applied to its cobalt surface. The word Emerge is scrawled in a cheerful script, surrounded by a sunny yellow design that radiates an almost comical sense of innocence.

But that's the problem, isn't it?

This little bottle looks so ordinary, so inconspicuous, so happily organic, that it only sharpens my suspicions.

"I'm so sorry about the mess I made last night," he says, glancing over at me from behind the wheel, apologising for the fourth time.

I shake my head. "You were sleepwalking. You didn't know what you were doing. I'm just glad you didn't hurt yourself."

"Still," he insists, his tone heavy with guilt. "It was late, and you had to clean without waking your parents. That couldn't have been easy."

I shoot him a wry smile. "I'm an expert at getting away with things while my parents are unconscious."

He reaches over and takes my hand. "What do you think we're going to find?"

"I don't know. Maybe I'm wrong. Hopefully, we're both crazy and your family is innocent."

"But what if they're not?" he asks. "And what if I grabbed the wrong bottle? What if this isn't the guilty one?"

I frown. "Maybe we should've taken the damn box."

"If the contents of this bottle reveal nothing malicious," he says, turning left at the roundabout leading out of Port Douglas "we might have to steal the box."

"I'm willing to help you with anything that'll give you peace of mind."

"So, where exactly does your friend live?"

"To be honest, I'm not sure," I reply. "She mentioned meeting us at Nusa on the esplanade, but she's pretty secretive about details. Doesn't like anyone knowing too much about her. She's funny like that."

"How did you meet her?" he asks me.

"I accidentally bumped into Ruliza at the Palm Cove Market. She was carrying these weird circular resin devices filled with crystals and metal shavings. I think she called them 'orgy night'."

He snorts. "I think you mean orgonite."

I snap my fingers. "That's it! Anyway, we started talking, and she gave me one. She said it keeps 'them' from listening."

"I'm surprised you haven't noticed all the orgonites around the retreat spaces. They're in almost every room. They're created and programmed to balance energy, protect against negativity, and promote a sense of wellbeing."

"Not to sound like your beloved Hauline Panson, but please explain!" I tease.

"Beloved my ass!"

I laugh. "She just hasn't met the right gay yet. I bet I can change her."

He snorts and continues his explanation of orgonite. "Depending on the intent, you combine the crystals and metals in a specific sacred geometrical configuration..."

"Ah!" I give him my very best understanding face. "That's makes sense."

"So, this Ruliza sounds very interesting," he says. "A scientist and a new ager."

"She's a character," I agree, sitting back in my seat and making myself more comfortable.

LCD Soundsystem's 'Oh Baby' plays over the car's stereo. I glance out my window, taking in the forever gorgeous view of the Coral Sea.

"I'm sorry if the tarot cards scared you," he says over the music.

I look back at him. "I will admit something weird is happening and drawing the same cards that many times shouldn't happen."

He nods.

"Let's focus on what we can understand," I suggest, holding up the bottle to the light. "Perhaps what's in here will answer some of our questions."

I look out my window again as we pass the turnoff to Aetherlys.

While we wait for Ruliza to make an appearance, I order beef rendang, and Rex goes with the chicken nasi goreng.

Thank God we sit under a shade sail because the sun beats down, and someone's newborn is making a feral noise.

Either pick that baby up and hold it or shove a tit in its mewling gob.

Just as I add more chilli sauce to my rice, a woman in her late twenties slides into the chair across from us. She dressed as if fearing a paparazzi onslaught—her head wrapped in a scarf, sunglasses hiding most of her face, and no jewellery visible.

"Hi," I greet her, putting down my fork. "Thank you so much for coming to see me. Do you want something to eat? I'll pay."

"Hi Jules," she says, looking as if she struggles not to remove her gloves and start biting her nails. "No, thank you. I only eat what I make myself. Can't trust people's intentions. Intent is everything you know. Energy. Vibrations. Everything rattles. Everything shakes. I'm shocked we've not come apart. What's really holding us together? Gravity? That's what they want you to think."

"I have something I need analysed," I tell her, ignoring Rex's amused stare. "Do you think you can help me?"

She nods her head. "I owe you. I must pay you back in full. Checks and balances. Everything must balance. Chaos is always rearing its head. Must keep discord in check."

Reaching into my pocket, I retrieve the bottle and discreetly slide my hand under the table. I knock twice and feel her gloved hand. I carefully place it in her palm.

"Please let me know what's in this oil," I say, my voice low. "It's really important we find out as soon as possible."

"Gas Chromatographer-Mass Spectrometer for essential oil composition," she replies, slipping the bottle into her bag. "Thin-Layer Chromatographer for adulteration."

I nod as if I understand her every word, though in reality, I plan on Googling it later, if I remember. For now, I just want to know what's in the bottle. "When will we know?"

"When I know," she tells me.

I snort under my breath. This is why I like her.

"Thank you so much, Ruliza," Rex says, giving her a grateful nod. "I really appreciate it."

She raises a finger slowly, then slides her sunglasses down just enough to meet his gaze. I notice her pupils dilating, despite the bright sunlight. "You're not alone..." she whispers.

Rex looks as if he's about to ask her what she means by that remark, but she stands up quickly and overturns her chair. Before I can react, she runs away from the table.

This draws the attention of those around us, and people turn in their seats, puzzled by the sudden commotion that isn't the screams of a child's tantrum.

Rex turns to me, confusion in his eyes. "What did she mean by that?"

I shake my head. "I don't know, but people are staring. They probably think we upset her."

He glances around, then looks down at his plate. A few people shoot us curious glances before returning to their meals.

I try to focus on my rice, but my appetite ran away with her, which is a damn shame, because this is fucking good food. "I guess we wait for her text."

He flicks his fork onto his plate. "Yep."

I turn my head towards him. "Expect the worst. That way, the best news will surprise you."

He takes my hand and holds it in his lap. "Since we're in Cairns, have you been to Kuranda yet?"

I shake my head. "No."

"Oh, we are so doing Skyrail then."

Walking through the Old Kuranda Markets feels almost surreal. The air is a vibrant mix of sizzling food and drifting incense, each scent tugging me in a different direction. One moment, the sun blazes down through the green canopy, and the next, a sudden shower cools everything in sight. Eccentric people fill every corner, no matter where I look.

Each stall is unique in countless ways—a treasure trove of the bizarre. I can't resist stopping to explore. I love searching through every shelf, unearthing hidden gems that have been tucked away, forgotten about, and are whispering to be rediscovered and appreciated.

"What's that?" I ask, getting distracted again, pointing to a small building nestled among gingers and lipstick palms. Soft, colourful lights glow from within, drawing my attention.

I walk over and look through the door.

A watermelon sized crystalline pyramid hangs delicately from the apex of a large copper pyramid in the centre of the treatment room. The copper frame gleams in the light.

"That's an iPyramid," Rex says, stepping up beside me. "We've got a room like this at the retreat. I'm not sure which model this one is using, but ours is called The Atlantis Stone. It's meant to harmonise energy and bring everything into balance."

"Kind of like orgonite then," I remark. "This looks ridiculously expensive."

He nods, a wry smile tugging at his lips. "It costs about as much as a bachelor's degree in the states."

I whistle.

"Mom and Dad sleep with one called Seraphim Dreaming suspended over their bed within a copper pyramid similar to this one."

"Oh..."

Another stall, overflowing with books, crystals, dream catchers, a large basket of sage bundles, and an assortment of other mystical paraphernalia, immediately draws my attention.

But none of that stops me in my tracks.

What really catches my eye is a handwritten sign that reads:

AURA PHOTOGRAPHS $35.

"I wanna get my aura photographed," I say, my gaze fixed on the sign.

"It's been ages since I had mine taken," Rex says. "I'm curious to see if it's changed any."

A woman with wild purple hair emerges from behind a tall glass display filled with raw crystals and wands. She looks like she's stepped straight out of a whimsical world where teacup dragons and gay dancing crockery are the norm.

"May I help you?" she asks, adjusting a thick bronze bangle on her wrist with a casual elegance before sucking on a long pipe that belonged to Madam Butterfly Dragon Bitch, and blowing smoke that smells of gummy bears.

"Yes," I answer, waving the smoke out of my face. "I'd like to have my aura photographed without developing lung cancer."

She snorts, motioning for me to follow her around the display case to Narnia. "I have my equipment set up back here in the corner. Just mind the faeries. They've been rather unmanageable today."

I nod my head, following her with Rex trailing behind. "Faeries noted. I shall mind the good folk."

She leads us back to a small booth draped in sheer, colourful fabrics. A black chair sits in the middle. The monitor next to it displays a swirling rainbow of colours, ready to capture the unseen energy each of us radiates.

"Have a seat." She motions to the chair. Her bracelets jingle softly. "Just relax and place your hands on the metal plates."

I do as she says, palms resting on the two cold, smooth plates fixed at the ends of each armrest. I glance at Rex, who stands just to the side of the camera, giving me a thumbs up.

"Ready?" she asks.

"Yep."

"Look at the red light."

A big flash teleports my vision to Mars. "Oh, my god!" I squint, head thrown back, moaning in ocular agony. "That was homophobic."

Rex snickers, and the woman laughs as the device whirrs softly.

In the meantime, I'm seeing sparkles and orbs. After a few moments of rapid blinking to get my sight back, the screen lights up with vivid streaks of colours. An image of me slowly appears on the monitor. Violets, blues, and soft pinks swirl together like a watercolour painting in motion.

"Oh," she says, her voice low with awe. "Such calm, intuitive energy. And so much compassion and love... just look at that intense spark of green right where your heart chakra is..." She trails off, studying the image.

I turn my head, staring at the colours all around me. They're beautiful. I glance at Rex, who steps closer to get a better look. "Looks like I'm made of cotton candy," I joke.

"Yummy," he licks his upper lip.

"I'll just print this off for you," she tells me.

I nod and hop up, placing seventy bucks near her keyboard for the both of us. "Thanks!"

As my photo prints, Rex eases into the chair, his tall, broad frame making the small setup seem almost comically cramped. He stretches his legs out slightly, crossing them at the ankles, trying to make himself comfortable.

"Here you go," she says, handing me my freshly printed aura photograph.

"Sweet," I reply, taking it and glancing down at the vivid swirls of violet, blue, pink, and that spark of green in my heart. It's pretty, but I turn my attention back to Rex.

He places his hands on the metallic plates, his expression rather excited. The camera emits another bright flash, and her equipment makes loud, sharp popping noises.

Sparks fly from the CPU, and the monitor goes dark. Rex yanks his hands away from the plates as the small space fills with the acrid scent only fried wiring can make.

"Oh, shit!" the proprietor cries, rushing over to check on him. "Are you okay? Did you get shocked? I don't know what could have gone wrong. This has never happened before."

"I'm fine," Rex turns to me, face filled with worry. "Did I just short circuit the universe or something?"

She inspects her computer, as I check his hands for any signs of burning. They look fine.

I turn to see her tap a few buttons. It looks like her setup is toast. Some kind of surge has destroyed her equipment.

I turn back to Rex and whisper, "This has been happening quite a bit."

I let him have his hands back and he stands up.

"I'm okay," he says.

"Sorry about your machine," I apologise.

She waves us away, looking as if she's about to cry.

We flee down the narrow cobblestone path like thieves.

Rex stops for a moment, resting his palm against the side of an empty stall, turning his head to look at me. "There is something really wrong with me," he says, colour draining from his face and he sways a little on his feet, nearly stumbling out of a thong as he takes a wobbly step towards me.

"Here," I motion towards a bench. "Have a seat."

As he sits down and leans his head back, I reach into my bag and pull out a bottle of water. I go to hand it to him, but he waves it away.

"No. I feel seasick."

Seasick?

I drop the bottle back into my bag and kneel at his feet, resting my hands on his knees. "Do you feel like you might throw up?" I ask, ready to dodge should he begin spewing projectile pea soup.

He shakes his head. "I don't think so."

"We did just have Indonesian... it isn't food poisoning, is it?"

"No."

I get up and sit down beside him. He leans over and rests his head against my shoulder.

"Let's just stay like this for a few moments," I say, lifting my arm behind his head and gently running my fingers through his hair. "Then we'll go sit in one of these air-conditioned cafes. You may just be too hot."

"I've caught the plague," he groans. "Ugh! I'm dying."

"Don't be so dramatic." I roll my eyes and gently tug at his hair.

He chuckles, kissing my throat. "I'm poorly."

A few moments go by and I notice the colour returning to his face. He sits up and takes a deep breath in and stands.

"I think I'm good," he says.

"Are you sure?" I ask.

He turns around and nods. "Yes." I stand up and he takes my hand. "Let's go get a smoothie. There's a shop by the photo gallery. You have to try the Dragon Fire."

"What's in it?" I ask.

"Dragon fruit, mango, ginger, and sugarcane."

"Sounds like a cavity."

"I can be your dentist."

"Only if you take your pants off."

"Of course. I'm not a doctor."

Beastly Eyes' 'Collector' starts with a low, growling bass—ominous, predatory—sliding beneath a sharp metallic beat that clicks chittering insect legs.

Lights pulse to the rhythm of a hundred excited hearts, and neon smoke slithers like spectral serpents around our ankles.

We are witches dancing with monsters—seduced by the ritualistic thrum, loving every wicked step that conjures iridescent shadows.

Rex's grin splits through the green and azure smoke. His dark curls are damp with sweat, clinging to his forehead as he throws his arms up and spins.

Just as the sinister synths slither in, I follow his lead—oily and sinuous—tension winding up with no release. I twist and turn like a priestess when the drop hits.

It's a dirty, distorted thump—like industrial machinery grinding under velvet.

He grabs my hands; we move to the off-kilter patterns of the punching drums, like reanimated corpses remembering how to use our joints.

Our laughter mixes with the snarling, twisted vocals.

He leans in, his voice barely audible over the throbbing sea of perfumed and glittering skin. "Check your phone," he says, before giving me one more twirl under the flashing lights.

Breathless, I reach into my back pocket and slip it out. I don't want to ruin this moment by tapping the screen. But curiosity wins. My thumb presses down, and the screen lights up. A single text message stares back at me.

Call me.

My stomach clenches. "Oh, shit," I hiss.

His breath is warm against my ear. "What?"

I grab his wrist and pull him through the writhing bodies. He follows without hesitation, his palm warm against mine, his breath still quick from the rhythm of the night. Bright lights flicker across our faces as we move through the crowd—past the bar and beyond the glow of sweat-slick dancers.

The cool night air hits me the moment I push through the doors. I don't stop until we reach the truck.

He unlocks the door and opens it for me without a word. I slide into the seat, and he shuts it after me before making his way around to the driver's side. As he climbs in, I tap the callback button, my pulse pounding in time with the distant thrum.

"Hello, Jules."

"Hi, Ruliza." I force a light tone. "What do you have for me? Nothing nefarious, I hope."

Silence.

"Ruliza?"

Rex looks at me, and I put the phone on speaker.

"I don't know what you're mixed up in, Jules. I'm going to give you everything you asked for, and then I'm ending this call."

My chest tightens. "O... Okay...."

"The ingredients are as follows," she begins, her voice steady and clinical. "Blue cypress, blue tansy, davana, frankincense, grapefruit, hyssop, jasmine, lavender, lemon, lemongrass, melissa, neroli, Roman chamomile, rose, Royal Hawaiian sandalwood, tangerine. All the highest quality, with zero adulteration."

Rex exhales. "That doesn't sound bad at all."

"And then there are the darker elements," she continues.

"Darker elements?" we ask at the same time.

"Angel's trumpet, belladonna, datura, henbane, mandrake—poisonous plants steeped in folklore. Herbs witches or oracles would use to leave their bodies and commune with their gods. These can be incredibly dangerous, hallucinogenic, and portal openers."

My hand shakes.

Rex reaches over, steadying my hand before I drop my phone.

"And then," she says, her voice dropping lower, "there's something else."

"What?" Rex asks.

"DNA."

"DNA?" My throat suddenly dry.

"From an unidentified source. It has no origin."

"No origin?" I repeat.

"What does that mean?" Rex demands.

"Exactly that," she answers. "No origin. It doesn't belong to human, animal, or anything traceable in the known database. It is... other."

The line beeps twice.

She either kept her word and ends the call, or Nelstro fucked up again.

My stomach twists. I meet Rex's gaze.

His grip loosens before he finally lets go of my wrist and leans back in his seat.

A thick silence settles over us.

"My family is poisoning me," he mutters. "Making me think I'm losing my mind."

I shake my head. "Your parents might have nothing to do with this. They may not understand what's happening either. Maggie may be behind it."

He exhales sharply, staring out the windshield.

"Can you remember when all of this started?" I ask.

He frowns, biting his bottom lip. "There was a party the day after I met you... I got drunk," his voice trails off. He shakes his head. "I can't remember. I think we were at the beach."

I lean over, resting my head against his shoulder.

"It's like something is blocking my memory. Like a thick blanket draped over everything, and no matter how much I pull at it, there's always more fabric."

My phone beeps. It's Ruliza!

> *One last thing, Jules. Your boyfriend needs more than an exorcism. Whatever is inhabiting him… it's dug itself in deep. Permeating. I know a person who may help him. I'll send through their details if he wants them.*

"You're not alone." That's what she means!

I look up at him, and my eyes widen in shock. I'm staring into four irises.

His usual amber eyes remain, but another set—glittering gold—emerge, splitting away from the originals like a reflection fracturing into something that shouldn't be possible.

I gasp, lift my phone, and snap a photo, the flash blinding him.

"Argh!" he growls, hands immediately flying to cover his eyes. "What the heck, Julian?"

I glance at my screen. His eyes look like headlights—bright, unsettling. Human eyes don't do that!

"You had four eyes," I say, turning the phone around to show him. "Your irises split into a pair of gold ones. Look."

He takes me phone. "You must have caught a glare from headlights or something."

I shake my head, taking my phone back. "I know what I saw. Plus, we're back here. There's no road, no cars coming back here." I show him the text from Ruliza.

He skims through it, and shakes his head. "This is actually happening."

"Yes." I set the phone down and take his hands in mine. "I just saw something inside of you looking at me. Whatever it was saw me, too. This is bigger than oils and herbs, Rex. You said you drive and don't remember where you go. You went to bed, woke up in your car with no memory and more than half a tank of petrol gone. People don't sleep-drive, Rex."

He's about to speak when something smashes into the windshield.

We jump—and then another, and another, and another.

We're being pelted by giant hailstones.

The headlights flicker on and off, and the radio blares to life, cycling through every channel.

"What is happening?!" I yell, panic rising in my chest as he wraps his arms around me, pulling me tightly against his chest, shielding me from the possibility of shattering glass.

The radio volume surges erratically, rising and falling in bursts.

"What is this force we struggle so hard against..."

Then—silence.

I lift my head, and he turns his, our eyes staring in disbelief. The windows, once riddled with fractures, are flawless—as if nothing had happened at all.

"What the fuck?" I hiss.

His eyes lock onto mine. "Why aren't you getting out of the car and running away?"

Did he really just ask me that?

"Because... you're my boyfriend."

His intense gaze softens.

I pick up my phone. "Do I tell her to send me their contact details?"

He doesn't answer. Instead, he pushes his door open just a crack—then yanks it shut, recoiling into his seat with a sharp inhale. His fingers fumble for the lock button.

THUNK!

My pulse spikes. "What? What is it?"

He turns to me slowly, his face pale. "We're surrounded by dead cockatoos."

I turn to look out my window. They are black cockatoos. Their bodies litter the ground. So many feathers splattered with blood under the lights.

"We need to meet this person," he says.

I quickly reply to Ruliza's text as he starts the engine, turns up the radio, and shifts into reverse.

A shudder runs through me as I feel the subtle bumps beneath the tires... grateful I can't hear any noise over Caroline Kingsbury.

Chapter Fourteen

My shirt sticks to my back, my lungs burn, each breath sharp and ragged as I tear through the bush, branches scratching at my arms. Every time I near a street, I slow just enough to scan for familiar cars before bolting across.

My heartbeat thunders in my ears, drowning out the sound of my pounding footsteps. Should I even be running like this? Is it safe? It doesn't matter. I have to get home. I have to get that key. I also should've knocked that mullet-haired bogan bitch off his bike and taken it. That would've made this a whole hell of a lot quicker.

My window of time is slipping by fast. Alexandra has already called my parents—I'm sure of it.

I round the last corner, and my house comes into view. The driveway is empty.

Cutting across the lawn, I vault over the flowerbed and drop to my knees in front of the door. I yank up the doormat for the spare key taped underneath. My hands tremble as I peel it free, jam it into the lock, and twist.

The door flies open, and I bolt inside, tearing up the stairs to my room.

I go straight for my dresser.

If you want to hide something, you put it where no one would think twice to look. My keyring. I snatch it up, fingers shaking as I sort through the keys. There you are!

I grab my wallet, spin around, and race back downstairs, straight to the garage.

I haul my scooter out through the side door, my pulse hammering in my throat. What if my parents pull up? What if Alexandra finds me?

What if the wee-woos speed in, flashing all blue and red for the neighbours to gawk as they cart my ass off to Straitjacket Junction?

I can just hear Yvonne now, out in front of her shop with a loudspeaker up to her lips. "Be on the lookout for a trim homosexual. He's all strange angles and sharp bones. We call him Twig, because a slight breeze could snap him in half. Anyway, he's my crazy stepson. I love him dearly, but he is delulu right now. He's also had a rather ethically fucked up heart transplant, so be gentle with his feelings. He's bitten people hard enough to draw blood and I'm afraid he rather enjoys the taste now."

I take off down the sidewalk at full speed as a kookaburra laughs.

Chapter Fifteen

JULY 2025

Dad's going to be pissed—no doubt about that—but there's no way in hell he'd ever agree to let me spend the night in Cooktown with Rex.

I can already hear his voice, sharp with suspicion. "Why do you two want to go to Cooktown?"

"Because Rex is being inhabited by another consciousness, and we need to see a shaman." Yeah, nah.

I lean forward and turn the volume up on the Spirit Nannies podcast we're listening to.

"She haunts the back room."

"Who?"

"The pencil sharpening nun."

"The what?"

"Old habits die hard."

I snort as they both laugh over the speakers.

"No. Really. When you walk by the back room, you see her there at the pencil sharpener, smiling as she's sharpening."

"That's so stupid!"

"Well, I didn't say ghosts are smart."

"True. If you weren't smart in life, you sure as hell ain't gonna be a genius in the Hereafter."

"Sharpening pencils for Jesus."

"Hallelujah! Number Two! The perfect balance of softness and hardness."

Rex chuckles and slows down.

I glance up to see a looming mountain of dark boulders ahead.

He eases over to a small viewing area and parks along the side. "I have to show you this." He points towards the towering mass of dark rocks that seem to swallow the sunlight.

Black Mountain National Park resembles something out of a dream—or maybe a nightmare, depending on your point of view. Huge black granite rocks pile one atop the other, stretching toward the sky like a giant frozen in time. Some of those boulders look bigger than a house.

"Wow." I step out of the truck. The heat hits me first, thick and oppressive, but the sight of those rocks distracts me from the discomfort. "It looks unreal."

"It has a reputation." Rex leans against the hood with his arms crossed. "Lots of stories about people going missing in there. They say it's a place of spirits."

I nod, unable to take my eyes off the jagged landscape. The way the rocks absorb the sunlight makes them look almost alive, like they're breathing heat back into the air. I catch myself longing to hear the sounds this place must make during a storm, when the wind howls through all those treacherous crevices. It looks like some giant beast with sharp teeth, ready to devour anything foolish enough to enter. "I can see why it's sacred. It feels like it's watching us... or they are."

Rex smiles at me. "Ready to keep going? We're almost there."

I stare past him. "Is that my dad's vehicle?"

"Shit!" He turns and looks. "Is it?"

I walk around the tail of the truck feeling like my heart's about to flee out my ass. I walk close enough to the other vehicle to read the license plate, and I start laughing at my paranoia.

Oh, thank god!

The first three letters don't spell ART.

"Well?" Rex asks. "Do I need to hop the barrier and take my chances in there?"

I turn back around. "False alarm. Sorry. Plus, you wouldn't last five minutes on those sharp rocks in them thongs."

He chuckles and climbs back into the truck.

I take one last look at those massive black stones before climbing back in as well. As we drive off, I glance back at the mountain—its shadow long and lingering, like a memory that will take a billion years to weather down.

We pay cash up front when checking into the Plumeria Resort and Spa just in case Big Daddy Dutton decides to have a look at his son's recent credit card splurges.

I've been texting back and forth with the shaman, Nadine, for the past three hours—feeding her all the details about what's happening, sharing nothing too personal about who Rex is. She seems to take me seriously—every message I send ticks all the right boxes for her. Plus, I have the backing of Ruliza's quick referral.

I show Rex my phone screen. "She wants to see us at six."

He looks at my phone and frowns. "What's she going to do?"

"Tie you to a bed and shove a cross up your ass." I deadpan.

I receive a snort. At least his humour is still intact. That's a good sign.

"She hasn't told me yet," I answer him for real.

He raises an eyebrow. "And you think this is going to work?"

"The cross will definitely cause some kind of reaction," I say.

He rolls his eyes. "Be serious."

I hesitate for a moment, then shrug. "If Maggie somehow did this to you through some kind of invocation, then there must be a ritual to undo it."

He flops back onto the bed, kicks off his thongs, and growls low in his throat.

I tell Nadine we'll be there on time, then set my phone down and curl up beside him. He wraps his arms around me, pulling me close, my face resting against his throat.

"What do you want to do to pass the time?" I ask.

He rests his chin on the top of my head. "I'm almost too afraid to go back out. What if a bunch of murder birds decide to dive-bomb us?"

"I don't think whatever this thing is wants to hurt your body," I say.

He shakes his head, his voice tense. "I'm afraid it might want to hurt you."

I remain silent. The thought had crossed my mind more than once.

"I really am shocked you haven't dumped me and left me to deal with this on my own," he whispers.

I smile. "I'm just waiting for you to write me into your will."

He wraps his legs around me and starts tickling my ribs.

"NO!"

"Accept my love!"

"No!"

"Accept my pure love!"

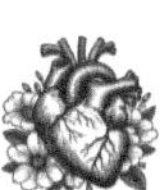

Nadine's Queenslander sits deep in the trees, wrapped in the scent of eucalyptus. Wind chimes clatter in the humid air, tangled among dried flora hanging from the eaves.

Rex and I exchange a look before stepping up onto her verandah. The old wooden planks creak beneath our weight, and it makes me nervous. The last thing I need is to go crashing through and wake up in some backwoods emergency department.

She meets us at the door—a middle-aged woman with copper-dark eyes and long, silver-threaded hair woven into a loose braid. She doesn't speak at first. Instead, she studies Rex, tilting her head slightly, as if listening to something only she can hear. "Welcome to my home," she finally speaks, making a gesture of welcome. "Enter freely and of your own will."

Well, that's fucking terrifying. Okay, Countess Dracula.

The inside of her home smells of mastic and crushed spices. A fire burns low in the hearth, casting strange, shifting shadows where there is only light. Even with the fire going, the room feels cooler than an April midnight in the Tennessee mountains. Shelves of glass jars seem to glow on their own. A large circular rug dominates the floor, its intricate patterns forming symbols I don't recognise.

"Please remove your thongs," she says, gesturing for Rex to sit in the middle of the rug.

He hesitates for only a moment, then does as she asks. He settles into the lotus position and makes himself comfortable.

"I need you to close your eyes," she says. "Breathe."

Rex exhales shakily and obeys.

"Somebody has been working you real good." She shakes her head.

She retrieves a mason jar of dark oil, dips a finger inside, and presses it to Rex's temples. Then she breaks off a long thorn from a nearby plant, its tip sharp and glistening. She dips it into the oil and carefully traces an intricate pattern across his forehead—each stroke deliberate, almost reverent—without breaking his skin. When she finishes, she leans in and exhales softly over the symbol.

And it glows.

"Who are you?" she whispers, her voice so low I have to strain to hear.

Rex inhales sharply. His fingers curl into fists. A low, keening sound slips from his lips.

I start forward, but Nadine lifts a hand to stop me.

His eyes open—but they aren't his eyes. Not really. His pupils dilate until his irises become nothing but thin rings of blue. Except his eyes aren't blue. They're amber.

"Something is inside him," she murmurs, pressing her fingertips lightly to his sternum. "It clings."

"Can you get it out of him?" I ask.

She doesn't answer right away. Instead, she reaches into another copper bowl and draws out a small vial filled with thick, red liquid. She tilts Rex's head back, places the vial to his lips, and massages his throat to help it go down.

"What's that?" I ask her.

"A cleansing. It will force that which is shrouded in darkness to step into the light."

Rex speaks, his voice deeper than I've ever heard it before. "We are the forge of Our own light, the herald of Our own darkness. They rise and fall at Our command." He doubles over, his hands clawing at his chest like he's trying to rip something out of himself.

Candles flare to life, their flames rising high. The floor trembles beneath us, the air thickens—charged like a storm about to crack the sky open.

His body seizes, his back arches. A guttural sound tears from his throat—not a scream, not entirely human.

His eyes snap open, and I stumble back.

They aren't just gold—they burn, radiant and molten.

The pressure in the room spikes, and my ears pop.

"Jesus!" I hiss in pain.

The flames bend toward him, drawn as if he's a whirlpool.

"This... this isn't possession," she says, almost in awe, beads of sweat gathering on her brow. "This is something else."

Rex rises until he's balanced on the tips of his toes, back arched, arms stretched behind him. He looks like he's trying to suck in a breath, his entire body trembling. When he speaks, his voice carries multiple layers—a canyon of reverberations echoing just behind his own. "I... remember..."

"What do you remember?" Nadine asks.

"I'm on the beach. It's night. There's a fire. I'm being held. Figures wearing sea green robes. Elaborate, mirror-like masks hide their faces. The air is so thick with smoke and incense. It's hard to breathe. I can feel hands all over me, touching me everywhere. Hands I can't see."

This is hard for me to listen to.

"A cup is being pressed to my lips. I don't want to drink, but they force me. I don't want to. It's sweet and gritty, spilling down my chin as I try not to swallow, but they force me."

My eyes sting as he literally balances on the tips of his toes.

"They are rubbing me with oil, tracing patterns that glow. I try to fight them. 'Mom!' I'm shouting. I'm yelling for my parents. 'Mom! Dad!' I'm unable to move. I don't see them. I can't move."

"You are safe, Rex. This is only a memory. It can't hurt you anymore. You are safe," she soothes.

"They are chanting. It sounds... I don't know. The sea is so loud. The wind is a roar."

"What else can you see? What else do you remember?"

"Light. So much light. It descends. A haze of gold, shifting and flowing over the waves, not solid but alive, moving like sand within an unseen current. It coils and slithers through the air towards me. I'm screaming. I'm screaming so loud as it enters both my mouth and nostrils, suffocating me."

My eyes widen as I watch his feet leave the rug.

He's screaming at the top of his lungs now, every muscle bulging, toes flexed.

Every vein in his forehead and neck is visible.

I catch something moving just under his face.

A second one!

He's floating...

"Help him!" I cry.

He drops to the floor like a crumpled doll.

I rush to him, and he practically wraps his arms around my waist, desperate to have something to hold on to.

Nadine looms over us; her face unreadable.

Her voice barely rises above a whisper. "I'm going to need the two of you to get the fuck out of my house."

Rex's breath comes in sharp gasps. "But I need your help."

"Ruliza said you'd help him!" I snap.

"That Chillagoe cave witch can go fuck herself," she says, rising to her feet. "Now get the FUCK out of my house."

Chillagoe cave witch? My nostrils flare, and my cheeks burn. I'm about to read her ugly ass house for filth, but Rex takes my hand and shakes his head. "Fine," I snarl, helping him to his feet.

He grabs his thongs, jaw tight with frustration, and he shuffles out.

I turn back to Nadine, something dark and instinctive rising in me, pushing the words past my lips before I can stop them from coming out. "If anything happens to him, I'll make sure you scream louder than he did."

Her eyes flash with something dangerous. She steps forward, and every candle in the room goes out at once, plunging us into thick shadow. "You think this is a game, boy?" she hisses. "You really want to piss off a shaman?"

The surrounding shadows shift as if they have weight, as if listening for a command to use their teeth to tear.

"This shit is real. And this shit is dangerous. You need to get the fuck as far away from that thing as you can."

I hold my ground. "What's in him? A demon?"

She lets out a slow breath, her shoulders trembling with the effort of restraint. "You entered of your own free will, Julian," she reminds me, her voice almost mournful. "Do not force me to take it from you. I'm trying so hard to remain good, but the night keeps whispering for me to come out and play."

I'm about to tell her to choke on a cork when something tugs sharply at my hair, and I flee through the door after Rex. "May your dildo always die right before the good part!" I yell as I slam it behind me.

After the cringe smiles at the post office, the gym is the only other place I can think of that has lockers. Members receive an assigned locker with their membership package, keeping access as long as they make timely payments.

Upon entry, I'm immediately assaulted by the smell of sweaty men. They turn their heads and their eyes follow me.

Okay. That's not creepy at all.

For the price of membership, surely to Christ they can at least afford a few oil diffusers from K-Mart.

A door closes, and a shower turns on.

My eyes scan the dull metal lockers until they find the number I'm looking for.

7!

I step up and stick the key into the lock.

It fits!

Of course it does.

For a split second, I hesitate.

What the hell am I about to find?

Something that will seriously fuck me up. That's what!

"Open it," Rex's voice whispers in my left ear.

I take a small breath and turn the key.

Click!

A deafening sound.

The metal door creaks open, revealing a plain manila folder and a cell phone.

I may as well be looking at a time bomb ticking down from ten.

"Take them," his voice orders.

Heart hammering, I snatch them up and quickly exit the room.

Terrible music blares from the speakers. Our generation really is cooked.

Heavy weights clang. Joggers pound on treadmills.

All the normal gym sounds one expects.

The tan guy at the counter makes eye contact with me and he smiles so big the skin around his eyes crinkle. I struggle not to squeak and run through the glass door.

As soon as I'm outside, I rush to my scooter. I need to find a place where I can borrow a charger so I can power up this phone. I need to hurry because I can smell another deluge moving in on the breeze.

A backpacker walks by me, talking on her phone. "I'm heading back now. Apparently, Bazza just formed. It looks to be tracking this way. I don't know. Is it early for this time of year?"

Well, fuck me. Where the hell did a cyclone come from? As if I don't have enough shit to stress about.

At least the library isn't too far. I'm not sure of the time, but I know they close their door at four.

I jump on my scooter as black cockatoos squawk their red-tailed feathers off.

When I open the library door, the smell of peppermint and eucalyptus immediately opens my sinuses. A lady I've not seen before looks up from her computer monitor and adjusts her Dame Edna glasses. "May I help you?" she asks.

"Hi. Sorry to bother you. Do you have an iPhone charger I can borrow? My battery has gone flat, and I need to find my friend." I lay the southern accent on thick. People gush over it and want me to read the phone book to them.

The look she gives me is sweet and thoughtful. Full of empathy and mild concern. "Of course. We should have one here. You'll have to leave your ID because people take them and don't give them back."

I laugh, letting my eyes tear up as I quickly think of a lie. "That's just it. He has my wallet in his backpack." I don't want to give her my ID in case someone has made phone calls around town to be on the lookout for a demon twink. "I can leave you my keys. Does that work?"

Her sympathy and empathy are rather overwhelming, and I instantly feel guilty for lying right to her concerned face.

She nods.

I nervously fish them from my pocket and hand them over.

She opens a drawer and drops them in.

She spins around in her chair and glides across the floor towards the cabinet in the corner. She opens the bottom drawer and rustles around inside for a moment and pulls something out.

A charger. Praise god!

"There are power points in the computer room," she says, coasting back across the floor, handing it to me.

"Thank you so much."

She nods. "You're welcome. And don't stress. Everything is going to be just fine."

Her tone puts me on edge. Far too reassuring.

"Thank you," I say.

Her petal pink smile is huge. "My pleasure."

I turn away and step back out into the humidity. I walk across the wooden floor to the computer room and open the door. Inside, the air conditioner is going, and the fans whirring on high.

Thank God the room's empty.

I take a seat at a desk where nobody can sneak up behind me and I can see everything in front of me should I have to run like hell. I plug the phone into the charger and put it aside, turning my attention to the folder.

Heart pounding, I skim the first page.

Something to do with an oil that was being used on Rex during his treatments at Aetherlys.

The name.

A list of ingredients.

I feel my eyes getting wider and wider as I read.

Some ingredients are poisonous.

Unidentified DNA?

What the hell does that mean?

Another paper documents strange, unexplained incidences in my handwriting and Rex's.

Birds, hail, and suicidal cockatoos.

Sleepwalking at my house.

Sleep driving.

Missing time.

Dissociation.

A horrible old woman.

Scary tarot readings with the same three cards showing up.

The Devil. The Tower. Death.

A photograph slips out, and I freeze.

My blood instantly runs cold.

It is Rex.

He is behind the wheel of his truck, and his eyes look like golden headlights.

He was a lighthouse in the dark.

My left eye twitches, and a sharp pain hits me between the brows. I squint and begin rubbing my temples. The pain slowly fades, and I shake my head. I pick up another piece of paper and my breath catches.

A handwritten letter from Rex to me.

BEAUTIFUL JULIAN,

I HOPE YOU NEVER HAVE TO FIND THIS, BUT I FEEL LIKE I NEED TO LEAVE SOMETHING JUST IN CASE THE WORST HAPPENS. SORRY FOR KEEPING SECRETS. I DON'T KNOW WHAT WE'LL FIND IN COOKTOWN, BUT I'M HOLDING ONTO HOPE THAT THIS NADINE WILL HELP WITH WHATEVER IS HAPPENING.

THANK YOU FOR STANDING BY ME AND NOT BREAKING UP. I NEED YOU TO KNOW THAT I LOVE YOU. I REALLY DO. IT MEANS EVERYTHING THAT YOU STAYED WITH ME WHEN I NEEDED SOMEONE THE MOST.

BUT IF SOMETHING BAD HAPPENS, PLEASE DON'T BLAME YOURSELF. IT'S NOT YOUR FAULT. I'M JUST SO TERRIFIED THAT I'LL BLACK OUT AND HURT SOMEONE. THE THOUGHT OF HURTING YOU... I CAN'T LIVE WITH THAT. I CAN'T WAKE UP AND FIND OUT I'VE DONE SOMETHING UNFORGIVABLE. THE GUILT OF NOT KNOWING WHAT I'VE DONE IS... IT'S MAKING ME CRAZY.

I'VE NEVER TOLD YOU THIS, AND I FEEL AWFUL FOR NOT SHARING IT SOONER, BUT YOU NEED TO UNDERSTAND. ONE MORNING, I WOKE UP WITH BLOOD ALL OVER MY HANDS AND CLOTHES. I DON'T KNOW WHERE IT CAME FROM OR WHOSE IT WAS, BUT THERE WAS SO MUCH OF IT.

I'VE HURT SOMEONE, JULIAN. AND IF THIS SHAMAN CAN'T HELP ME, I'LL TAKE CARE OF IT MYSELF.

YOU'RE GOING TO THINK I'M A HORRIBLE PERSON. MAYBE EVEN SELFISH, BUT I WILL NOT RISK YOU. I'LL TRY TO DO EVERYTHING I CAN TO KEEP YOU SMILING. I'LL SNEAK AWAY WHEN YOU'RE ASLEEP.

JUST KNOW THAT I LOVE YOU. YOU DID EVERYTHING YOU COULD, AND I'LL BE FOREVER GRATEFUL FOR YOU. DO NOT FEEL GUILT.

WITH MY HEART IN YOUR HANDS,

REX

I struggle not to scream and chew the letter to pieces. Here's his suicide letter! I'm probably holding the last thing he ever wrote. Tears sting my eyes, and I read it over and over.

Flashing shards of memory cutting through the thick fog. It's coming back to me. Everything!

The thunder.

Drops of rain on my bare skin.

The feel of him on top of me and inside of me.

A key entering a lock made just for it.

The stabbing pain in my chest.

"I'm sorry, Julian."

I whip my head around.

I'm alone.

Outside humidity fogging the windows, and I see a love heart being drawn by an invisible finger right in front of me.

I gasp as the phone vibrates, and I turn to it. It has reached 5%—just enough power to turn on.

"Pick it up."

I hesitate before doing so.

The lock screen comes up immediately. No password. Just swipe to unlock.

I swipe

There is a missed call and one voice message.

I stare at it, my finger hovering over the play button.

"Listen."

I tap and put it to my ear.

A sound.

Buzzing. Whining. Like a dental drill. But graver.

Deep creaks and pops of something that sounds like wet sticks breaking.

"Just look at how his heart glows. Reminds me of a sunlit pomegranate seed."

Oh, God!

Am I listening to the sound of Rex being pulled apart?

"I knew Rex wasn't strong enough. I told you he was weak and would bring about nothing but disaster. He's ruined everything!"

"We have to put his heart in Julian now. Just listen to how it beats."

It was!

I force back bile from what I'm hearing. Sweat ran down my back.

"There is darkness in the boy. He lost his mother at a young age. How do we know he won't end up the same? It should have been a girl."

"Well, out of everyone at the ceremony, Rex was chosen. We will put his heart in Julian. Have you even looked up at the sky? It isn't just flickering now, it's empty. That's a sign."

"Stealing my oil. Running away to Cooktown. Splattering his brains all over that redneck hillbilly bogan's yard. I can still smell it. Oh, he's got a nerve..."

"We must do this now, or we will lose decades of—"

"Wait! What is this? His phone. It's recording!"

"That motherfucker... he's still here! Rex!"

"Get the eucalyptus and the black tourmaline!"

The voice message cuts out.

I sit frozen, the phone still in my hand, pressing against my ear hard enough to hurt. That was Maggie and Suzannah.

My heart pounds in my ears.

No. Rex's heart pounds in my ears. They had given me his heart. My dead boyfriend's heart beats in my chest. The golden masks. Some twisted, fucked-up ceremony. Something had entered him, inhabited him. They had done this. They had done this to him on purpose.

Inside my head, I scream.

THEY PUT HIS HEART IN ME!

The wind picks up and the glass window in front of me cracks.

They gave me my dead boyfriend's heart.

The sky is empty...

I kick back, the wheels of the chair sending me sliding away, the cracks spreading, snaking through the glass as if under intense pressure, cutting through that love heart.

And that thing inside him.

Not a demon.

Something far worse.

The sky is empty...

Whatever was in him is now inside of me.

"You must've been so scared... and you were all alone..." I whisper.

The sky is empty...

"I'm so sorry, Julian."

A sudden blast of thunder shakes the room to its framework. The windows rattle in their frames, trembling with the force of the sound. Overhead, the lights flicker once, twice—then steady.

A cry rises from the indigo depths. A pained moan slips from my lips, and then, all at once, a microburst. Every glass window around me explodes outwards. The roar of the ocean drowns my scream.

Chapter Seventeen

July 2025

We sit atop Grassy Hill on a picnic table, overlooking the bay. In the distance, a brilliant flash of violet lightning illuminates the night sky and spears the sea. Thunder rumbles across the dark waves, the vibration causing the hair on the back of my neck to rise. The wind picks up, carrying the sharp scent of salt. Branches above us sway and creak, speaking to one another in their secret language those who can't photosynthesise can no longer understand.

I convinced Rex to come up here after cooling off in the resort pool. He wanted to stay in the room and mope after our swim, but I tell him he might as well brood with a view.

"We'll figure something else out. Maybe some mystic in Kuranda can help."

He holds my hand as we watch the town's lights flicker in the darkness. I lean in, and rest my head on his shoulder.

Another low boom of thunder and he finally speaks. "I'm sorry for dragging you into this. It was a wasted trip, and now you're probably going to get into trouble—for nothing."

I press my cheek against his shoulder, nuzzling it like a cat. "This trip wasn't a waste. We learned the supernatural is real. Getting into trouble is the last thing on my mind."

He sighs and tilts his head, resting his cheek against the top of my head while giving my hand a squeeze. "I wouldn't blame you if you stepped back... if you decide to call it quits."

I hesitate before asking, "If the roles were reversed, would you?"

A heavy silence stretches between us before he finally answers, his voice quiet. "I don't know. I'd like to think I wouldn't... but any sane person would have run screaming."

I pull away, and he meets my gaze. My eyes lock onto his, searching, before my fingers trace the contours of his face. His jawline feels endless, sharp and strong beneath my touch.

"If I'm going to get in trouble," I murmur, tracing the edge of his bottom lip, "we might as well make it worthwhile."

He cups my cheek, his thumb stroking my skin. "And what exactly do you have in mind?"

I smirk. "Isn't there a quilt in the backseat?"

He nods. "Yeah."

I hold his gaze, my smile deepening. "Drape it over this picnic table and make love to me."

His eyes widen. "Are you serious?"

I grin. "Just look at where we are. No matter what happens next, we'll always have this moment."

"Will it make you happy?" he asks.

I nod. "Yes. It's what I want. Will it make you feel better?"

Without another word, he lets go of my hand and takes off, running toward the truck. I laugh as he practically dives into the backseat, fumbling for the blanket before sprinting back.

Even in the dark, there's no missing his erection.

I stand and step down to help him spread out the quilt. It's king-size, so we keep it folded in half for extra cushioning against my back.

"Should anyone climb the hill, I'll have just enough time to pull out and jump off the ledge," Rex says.

I laugh.

"Besides, we're tucked far enough away from the lighthouse and lookout. These trees and bushes will provide plenty of cover as we dive into the truck."

I turn my back and start peeling off my clothes, carefully placing each piece on the wooden bench before getting as comfortable as I can on the table. The quilt is warm against my back from being in the truck all day.

I watch as he strips his clothes off, and I've seen no one undress as fast as he does. In fact, he's the only guy I've ever seen do it—at least, in real life.

The wind blows, and a few drops of rain land on my sensitive skin.

He's now standing in front of me. His large cock harder than a steel pipe.

He steps up and looms above me, his hair billowing in the wind. "Are you sure?"

I nod and his confident hands roam over me, gentle but insistent, touching me in places that make me squirm under him in delight.

I can hear music and lift my head. It was Cigarette's After Sex singing 'Apocalypse'. "Did you turn the car stereo on?"

He nods as the trees sway even more; his fingers tracing patterns across my skin. Our bodies move together, synchronised, as the storm creeps closer, sending a shiver down my spine.

Our lips meet and the world around me melts away, leaving only the sound of our breathing, the creaking of the picnic table beneath us, and my heart beating in my ears.

With every passing moment, the passion between us grows. His touch becomes more insistent, his lips burning with a fierce intensity, and I feel myself losing control.

I hear the soft pop of a plastic cap and lift my head. He's holding a small bottle of intimate oil, his eyes fixed on mine.

I take it from him without a word, pour a generous amount into my palm, and reach for his dick. My hands glide over him, warm and slow, cradling his hard length and girth between my palms. He shudders above me, a tremor that travels through both of us, deep and electric.

He positions himself. "Are you sure?"

I nod. "Yes."

"Tell me stop and I will," he tells me.

I smile. "Thank you."

I surrender everything as we slowly merge.

The pain is sharp and sweet, his body becoming one with mine, filling me, making me hiss like a serpent and hum like a honeybee.

We move in a slow, sensual grind, and every thrust of his hips makes me feel like I'm about to vibrate into another dimension.

No one has ever touched me like this—like he wants to ruin me and worship me all at once.

This is the best I've ever felt, and then he hits it.

I want to kiss him and smack him in the same breath.

A sharp pinch that makes me gasp into his mouth. "Oh, my God!"

A spark ignites, starting a fire that spreads. Every pleasure nerve tingles. Tiny explosions sending shockwaves through my body.

"There!" I cry against his citrus scented throat, breathing him in. "Right there. Don't you dare stop."

He chuckles.

"Oh, god," I hiss, nipping his bottom lip as he does it again and again and again.

That's all the encouragement he needed.

"I love you."

Hearing that, he grows harder, if that's possible. His thrusts became faster and faster.

Our sweat-slick skin sliding smoothly together as I gaze past him. The Tempest constellation above us looks as if it's flickering... and then that region of heaven goes dark.

Has a cloud merely obscured it from my view?

"Love me, love me, love me..."

"I do."

His mouth finds mine as smooth and continuous streams of his warm semen fill me and a strange, subtle pressure in my chest—just a slight squeeze at first, almost like a tight hug from the inside. But it deepens quickly, turning into a sharp, gnawing pain that spreads like electricity through my ribs.

My breath hitches, panic rising as the world around me seems to blur as I cum harder than I ever have. It feels so good, but I'm too nauseous to appreciate it. My heart races, not with excitement or pleasure, but with a terrible, crushing fear.

I can't catch my breath, and every second feels like I'm suffocating, drowning in a sea of panic I can't escape.

Rex's voice—panicked, distant—calls my name, but it's miles away, as if the space between us has stretched into something vast and unreachable.

My palms press against his slick chest. I must say something, but the words vanish the moment they leave me.

I'm falling—plunging through lances of light, sharp and blinding.

Strong arms catch me, lifting me as if I weigh nothing at all, only a dandelion seed.

And then... music...

Are those wings I hear flapping?

"I love you..."

The world shakes.

Chapter Eighteen

DECEMBER 2025

The sweet scent of frangipani tickles my nose.

Disoriented and sluggish, I pry my eyes open and push myself upright; the cool bamboo sheets slip from my bare shoulders.

My vision swims in the dim light, and I blink several times, struggling to chase away the lingering blur of sleep.

I take in my surroundings—Rex's bedroom.

I'm in his bed.

How did I get here?

Wasn't I at the library?

The rose quartz lamp blooms to life, its soft pink glow illuminating the space. Across the room, his vintage CD player from the early 90s crackles with static before dissolving into the piano melody of 'After Dark' by Mr. Kitty.

Pressure—building in my ears as though I'm quickly ascending a mountain—followed by a sharp ringing in my left.

A loud POP splits the silence, a flash of azure light searing my vision.

I moan.

A sound caught between pain and happiness.

Rex stands at the foot of the bed.

I reach out to him. "Are you okay?"

He shakes his head.

Thunder rumbles.

"Are you in pain?" I ask, stretching my hand further into the rose gloaming. "Can I help you?"

He flickers as he crawls onto the mattress, into my waiting arms. Tears sting my eyes, spilling down my cheeks as I pull him close, holding him as tightly as I can.

He feels weightless—like cold steam and shimmering light, slipping through my grasp yet still here.

A sob tears through me, then another, until I'm shaking in his embrace. "They put your heart in me."

"I thought I could protect you," his ghostly voice stirs a deep ache inside me. "But I can't protect anything at all."

I cling to him, terrified he will slip away—become nothing more than air between my fingers.

"My heart still beats..." He presses a kiss to the top of my head. "I'm the only thing holding it back... but I'm getting weaker."

His lips are warm.

Memories flare—unfolding like a movie playing in my mind.

Him driving down Grassy Hill... the truck sputtering to a stop... his hand pulling a gun from the glovebox... him lifting me into his arms, holding me close... running from people chasing.

A house beyond swaying palms.

Rain.

His voice, raw and trembling, telling me how much he loves me.

Hands reaching for him from the parting gloom.

Every minuscule shard of broken glass scattered in the darkness of my foggy mind pulls itself back together, drawn by his gravity, until it becomes a mirror again.

And then—BOOM.

Eyes wide.

Mouth gaping.

Tears dripping from my chin.

"Where did you get that gun?" I yell, struggling not to scream at him. "I'm so mad at you! Why? Why did you do that?"

His eyes shimmer with crystalline tears as I pull him back into my arms.

"I killed you," he whispers, his voice layered with guilt. "Killing myself was the only way I could stop it."

I squeeze my eyes shut, my chest tightening. "What do you mean, you're the only thing holding it back?"

"Because I'm still with you," he says, pressing his hand against my chest. "Whatever has taken up residence in our heart can't fully inhabit you while I'm still here."

Our heart.

"They're trying so hard to purge me, but all it can hope to do is slip through in brief outbursts."

"I think... in one of those outbursts, I destroyed the library," I whisper.

"And that's why I brought you here. It'll be the last place they think to look for you."

I fall silent for a moment. Had he possessed me?

"My parents put something in me against my will. They did this to me on purpose. They channelled and called it through, and now it's in you. I don't want to scare you, Julian, but you are going to have to make a choice."

"What is it?" I ask him. "I need to know."

He looks at me. "I don't know what it is, but it made me do terrible things. I still can't remember."

"How do I stop it?"

His head turns away from me, drawn towards the closet door. "Inside you will find a shoe box on the top shelf, left side."

I rise from the bed and approach the closet.

I reach out to grasp the knob, but the door opens on its own. A breath of sweet-scented air slips out, brushing against my skin. Then, with a quiet hum, the light turns on.

Without hesitating, I step inside. Sure enough, there's a shoebox on the top shelf. Standing on my tiptoes, I reach up, grip it with both hands, and pull it down. As I turn, I see him standing in the doorway, looking at me with incredibly sad eyes. He steps aside and I carry the box over to the bed and place it down. Lifting off the lid, I set it aside. Inside, I find ruffled black and gold tissue paper. Pushing it away, my eyes land on the gleaming metal of a small handgun.

I turn and look at him. "What's this?"

"The way you end it." He walks closer.

"What?"

Tears sparkle down his cheeks. "I'm sorry," he says, taking another step forward. "But you're going to have to kill yourself."

My eyes widen. "What are you saying?"

"You have little time," he says, glancing towards the doorway. "If whatever they called into our heart takes you over completely, we can never be together. It will lock you away and I can never reach you."

I look from him to the gun and then back to him.

"Do this," he says. "Because I can't do it for you, even though every fractal of my soul is telling me to bash your head in. I can't bring myself to hurt you, even if it means saving you. It must be your choice."

Thunder rumbles directly over our heads.

I draw in a deep breath. "You are giving me permission?"

His bottom lip trembles. "Yes," he whispers.

I feel myself beginning to smile as I reach for freedom from this nightmare, drawing it closer to me. With a steady hand, I pick up the gun. Steel flashes in the overhead light as another boom of thunder sounds. "You won't hate me?" I ask him, removing the safety with a soft click.

He shakes his head. "How can I hate? I love you."

"Will you hold me?" I ask.

He nods and climbs onto the bed, settling with his back against the headboard. Gently, he pulls me against his chest and wraps his arms around my waist. His breath is crisp against my ear as he whispers, "I'll never let you go. We'll walk out of here together, leaving all of this behind us."

I look at the gun in my hand. "Will it hurt?"

The song we'd made love to comes from his stereo.

"It was so fast. I don't remember falling."

I lift the gun. "Guide my hand and I'll pull the trigger."

His luminous hand forged from crystalline breath, gently grips my own, guiding it to where to place the barrel of the gun so it will be quick and correct.

"I have you," he assures me. "And I'm not letting you go."

I close my eyes, my finger on the trigger. Just as I'm about to happily pull it, there is a faint pulsing, a tremor. Behind my eyelids, the darkness fills with a light. Soft at first, and then grows with a blinding intensity as it violently rushes right at me.

Boom.

Boom.

Boom.

I open my eyes, and I'm kneeling between his legs.

The gun is still in my hand.

Rex slumps forward, smoking, glowing holes burn through his chest, a pearlescent fluid seeping out in slow, shimmering rivulets.

The gun slips from my grasp. I lunge toward him, hauling him into my arms as liquid light spills from the corner of his mouth, cool and impossibly bright against my skin.

His head lolls back.

"Rex?"

"I love you... Julian..."

He reaches up and gently caresses my wet cheek before dropping his hand.

I shake him. "REX!" What the fuck did I do? "Rex?" I cry, cradling him. "Rex! Please don't leave me. Not again!"

He melts away, slipping between my fingers as if he is nothing more than fading mist.

"REX!"

Something sucks every molecule of oxygen from the room.

I claw at the sheets.

Another piece of me gone.

The ceiling sounds like something is trying to rip it off.

A rush smashes through the air like a roaring tidal wave, and the surrounding walls crack inward.

"WHAT THE FUCK DID I DO?"

The light above flares bright and the bulb shatters.

"REX!"

Strong hands grip my arms from behind, and I scream into the dark.

Chapter Nineteen

July 2025

The small white building stands stark and solitary beneath a storm-churned sky. Its green sign, usually welcoming, is barely visible in the flashes of lightning that slash through the clouds. The wind howls down Carlotta Street, whistling through the railing slats and causing the hanging sign to creak on its fastenings.

Sheets of rain pelt the vet's roof, drumming with a relentless fury, and the light inside is faint, flickering—a pale glow behind the blinds like a dying lantern. The massive rocks out front glisten, their surface slick and shining like the backs of sleeping beasts. Water cascades down the steps in rivulets, pooling near the sidewalk.

The blue and white handicapped signs tremble on their posts, bending slightly with every gust. The two white unmarked vans sway side to side. Thunder cracks so loud it shakes their windows.

Inside the clinic, the power goes out.

"SHIT! MOTHERFUCKER!"

Rattling and the slamming of a drawer too full.

"Can't do piss all in bumfuck FNQ. Every time a little breeze blows a twig out of a tree, every goddamn light goes out! It's not like we're trying to perform a lifesaving surgery here!"

"Calm yourself, Suzannah."

"I AM CALM!"

The backup generator hums from the rear, sending jittery light through the cracked overhead fixtures. In the centre of the surgical room, beneath a swaying lamp and a ring of powdered obsidian and sea salt, a young man lies naked on the steel examination table.

Julian.

His chest rises shallowly, breath tethered to the veil between life and something much older.

Maggie calmly stands at his head.

Suzannah angrily stands at his feet.

Both have their hands extended over him, chanting under their breath.

Doctor Gregory Vines—Julian's father—stands gloved at his son's side. He looks less like a doctor now and more like a priest in scrubs, sleeves rolled, stethoscope discarded. His eyes gleam behind protective goggles, and a silver scalpel trembles slightly in his hand.

"You better not disappoint me, boy," he whispers. "Far too much is riding on this."

"Ready, doctor?" Maggie asks.

He nods.

She places her hands on Julian's temples and whispers an incantation. Julian exhales as she rubs the oil across his brow.

Her words keep oxygen flowing through his system.

Doctor Vines slices cleanly down Julian's sternum.

The smell of antiseptic mingles with hot copper and bees wax.

He moves with practiced speed, years of muscle memory guiding his hands through the Macarena of human anatomy. The bone saw, once meant for mastiffs, shrieks as it splits through his son's breastbone.

Maggie anoints the wound with poppy oil and datura ash.

The rib spreader cranks open the chest cavity with a wet, hollow creak.

With mechanical precision, she inserts the tubing—rubber hoses lined with dolphin skin and sea glass—into the vena cava and aorta. She begins the hand-pump circulation as Suzannah murmurs to the blood in the basin, keeping it oxygenated with each breath and chant.

Doctor Vines reaches in and disconnects his son's weakened and ischemic heart.

A furnace gone cold.

It comes free with a sickly squelch, like roots pulled from the wet earth. He drops it into a bowl carved from lapis and lined with blue sea salt.

It continues to beat—once, twice—before going still forever.

Maggie drapes a rune embroidered cloth over it.

"The heart of hearts," he commands.

Maggie reverently opens the cooler. Mist rolls out, smelling of a thousand damask roses carried on deep ocean currents.

Rex's heart rests inside, glowing like a rose red moon.

She reaches in with her gloved hands and picks it up as if it were made from the rarest glass. She carefully turns and places it in his waiting hands.

As he places it into Julian's chest, the lights flicker.

Suzannah growls.

He works swiftly, suturing the atria, and ventricles with golden wire soaked in ichor.

The work... delicate.

The heart feels warm—too warm—impatient to live again.

"TIME!" he calls.

Maggie steps forward, holding a slender crystal rod. She raises it toward the ceiling where thunder cracks again, then presses the copper tip to the base of Julian's sternum.

The jolt is silent, but his back arches off the table.

Then again.

Another convulsion.

The heart flutters.

Stills.

Then beats.

Once.

Twice.

A beautiful and perfect rhythm catches.

Doctor Vines casts his bloody hands up to the ceiling, tossing his head back as lightning flashes beyond the window behind him. "IT'S ALIVE!"

All the caged dogs in the back room howl.

Maggie chuckles.

Suzannah grumbles under her breath. She walks over and kicks the door to the kennel. "SHADDUP!"

Silence follows.

Doctor Vines wires the sternum shut, then sews the skin closed.

Maggie anoints the stitches with a mixture of blood, crushed myrrh, and mandrake.

"Now we need to get him to Cairns," Suzannah says. "We have contacts there that will do the rest, doctor."

Doctor Vines gazes down at his beautiful work of art. "He really looks like his mother. I hope this is worth the price."

"It will be," Suzannah confirms. She turns away and begins collecting all the tools. "Decades of labor will bring reward."

Maggie tenderly wraps Julian in a woollen blanket.

"What will you do with his heart?" Doctor Vines asks them. "Burn it?"

Suzannah looks at Maggie.

"We will place it in Rex's chest, along with honey and precious resins, before sewing it up." Maggie answers him.

Suzannah nods, "We're not barbarians." She drops everything into a metal bin.

"We just need for you to sign this form. That way, everything will look all pretty and legal, Doctor Dearest," Maggie smiles.

He removes his blood-soaked gloves and takes the pen and paper from her.

Suzannah picks up the bowl containing Julian's heart and carries it from the room.

"The Duttons knew the risks," Maggie tells him, reaching out and running her fingers through Julian's dark hair. "And they will be rewarded for their great sacrifice... as will you. As will we all."

Doctor Vines hands over the papers. She eyes each dotted line and gives him a big grin. "Please excuse me," she says, turning away from him. "Stay with your son. The ambulance will arrive shortly to take you both to Cairns." She exits the room, walks down the little hallway and into the room where Rex's body lies open on a table under a light. She closes the door behind her and leans back against it.

"His soul is still here," Suzannah hisses.

Maggie nods. "I know. But he won't be able to do anything."

"The phone call..."

"Nothing to be done about it. The great work is almost finished. Now we wait and see." She glances up in time to witness Suzannah slapping the remnants of Rex's face.

"You gotta nerve! If you weren't dead, I'd..."

Both flinch as something loud slams into the metal cabinet drawer across from Rex's feet, the sharp clang reverberating through the room. They immediately turn to look. A deep, jarring impact—like the blow of a phantom fist—has left the drawer deeply indented.

They both look at each other.

"Get the honey."

"Get the myrrh."

Chapter Twenty

JULY 2025

My world is a watercolour left out in the rain. Every soft edge melting into the other.

The sharp scent of antiseptic and bleach stings my nose. My tongue feels scratchier than a cat's against the roof of my mouth.

I shift—wincing because every breath is raw and unfamiliar. My breath is shallow, each inhale a little harder than the last.

My chest feels heavy, like a burning weight is in it.

I try to move my hand, but my limbs have forgotten how to work together. After a few agonising moments, my fingers twitch, finally finding the edge of the blanket. I tug, the rough fabric dragging over my skin, and then, slowly, I turn my head.

I blink a few times, trying to clear sleep from my eyes.

The white walls are so sterile, so empty, and that beeping is driving me insane.

"Julian?" A distant voice calls my name with such care, as though afraid I might shatter if touched too roughly.

I turn toward the voice, and I try to speak, but only a croaky rasp comes out. I feel like I have sandpaper in my mouth.

The figure leans forward, a silhouette, and slowly, the fog lifts—just enough for me to make out Yvonne's concerned face. Her eyes are red-rimmed, her lips pressed tight like she's holding something back. "Sweetheart," she whispers, her voice softer now. "You're okay. I'm here. The procedure went better than we could have hoped."

Procedure? Her words make little sense to me. What procedure? I try to ask, but all that comes out is a broken whisper, barely a sound.

Her soft hand brushes my cheek. "You had a heart attack, Julian," she says, and I stare at her, waiting for her to say something else. But her words hang in the air, and they settle into me like a brick dropped in water.

My chest tightens, the pressure building, and I feel the familiar weight of panic rising.

"No... no," I whisper.

I try to sit up, but she gently presses me back down.

"You've had a lot of medication," she says. "You need to rest, honey. Let the doctors take care of you."

I want to ask her more, but I can't form the words. I feel disconnected from my body, like I'm floating just above it, watching everything happen from a distance.

I don't feel like me.

Something is missing.

I lose track of time.

I'm kept medicated, my body held hostage in this room.

The doctors tell me it's keeping me calm, to let my body heal, but their eyes are not matching their words.

Their eyes hold fear.

But I'm not calm, not at all. I'm numb. Trapped between waking and sleep, between the world I remember and the one that's now crumbling around me because my questions are not being answered.

"Where's Rex?" Every time I open my eyes, I ask. "Where is Rex?" No one will answer me. "Where's Rex?"

My stepmother's face twists with something unreadable whenever I ask. She changes the subject. She strokes my hair and whispers how glad she is that I'm getting stronger.

Father finally visits. "Hello, son." He's been absent.

The space between him and my stepmother stretches wider each time I blink.

He doesn't say much. He just sits beside my bed, his eyes distant and unreadable. His exhaustion shows on his face, and he grips the chair's edge as if clinging to something he doesn't want to lose. "I'm glad you're still with us, son," he says eventually, his voice rough with something more than tiredness.

I ask about Rex. But he doesn't answer me, just looks away.

When next I open my eyes, the Duttons are in my room. I am so happy to see them. Finally, I'm going to get to see Rex!

They're speaking to my parents, but their eyes constantly flick towards me, like I'm something fragile they're too afraid to touch.

I try to speak again, to ask again where Rex is, but my words get lost in the drips of medicine and the sweet scent of oils.

"Julian," Mrs Dutton says, her voice reminding me of sunlight through honey, but there's something darker at the core. I can feel it. "You've been through so much. We're here to support you and we're so happy you're going to make a full recovery."

I want to scream. I need to know where Rex is.

They all look at me like I'm broken, as if I'm not supposed to ask anything.

And then I drift off again, my mind beginning to dream again for the first time since waking up.

I'm standing barefoot on the cold sand of a desolate beach. The sky above is ink-black, bruised with thunderclouds, and the sea before me thrashes and writhes. Wind tears through the air, sharp and relentless, whipping my clothes and stinging my face with salt.

I turn—something pulls my attention—and far in the distance, I spot a lone figure standing atop a jagged, towering rock. The stone looks like a broken tooth jutting out of the earth, slick with sea spray and menacing. The wind howls, but still I can make out their frantic gestures. They are waving wildly, their arms slicing through the storm-dark air, trying to catch my attention. Then they point—urgently, desperately—out toward the sea.

I follow their gaze.

From the horizon, a colossal wave rises. It grows, higher and higher, an impossible wall of black water crowned with foam, looming like a mountain torn loose from the ocean floor. Time seems to stall as I stare at it, frozen, the roar just beginning to reach my ears.

And then I hear him. "Run, Julian! Run!"

It's Rex!

"Rex?" I step forward, but I can't reach him. Something is holding me back. An invisible wall I can't penetrate. I try again, fighting against the wind, but the harder I try, the worse the wind blows.

The roar only gets louder and louder. The ground under my feet is trembling.

I am overshadowed by darkness.

"JULIAN!"

I wake up breathless, my heart racing.

Doctors explain that I need to rest. They want me to recover, they say, but I don't feel like I'm recovering. I feel like I'm being kept weak deliberately. They're keeping me drugged because every time I have an outburst, they literally flinch as though I'm about to kill them.

Every time I close my eyes, I hear Rex's voice—so faint, so close, but always out of reach.

And then, they tell me. "Sweetheart," my stepmother says, her voice barely a whisper. "After finding you help... Rex took his life."

I stare at her like she was telling the funniest joke in the world.

"He didn't survive. He's gone."

Rex wouldn't kill himself. He would never do that. "Shut up," I whisper, shaking my head. "Just shut up."

"He's gone, Julian," my father's voice cuts through the white noise.

And then Alexandra tells me something that makes the world break. "Your heart was damaged beyond anything surgery could... you needed a transplant, and Rex's heart was a perfect match."

My father curses under his breath.

"We gave you our son's heart."

I put my hand to my chest, feeling the vibration beyond flesh and bone.

It's Rex's heart.

They put his heart in me.

I gasp for air, my chest tight.

I can't breathe.

Rex is gone.

The very thing keeping me alive had belonged to him.

What had we been doing? I can't remember. I can't remember anything!

I get out of bed, my father frantic, his hands on me, trying to push me back down. The machines shriek, IVs rip free, and blood spatters the sheets. Objects clatter to the floor, crashing, breaking.

None of it matters. I have to see. I stagger to the mirror.

A pale, crimson-eyed wraith stares back.

My hospital gown pools at my feet, exposing the fresh, angry wound carved down my chest. It pulses red, raw—alive. It looks like they had stapled me back together.

His heart is beating inside me.

REX IS DEAD, AND HIS HEART IS BEATING IN MY CHEST.

This is the reason I don't feel like myself. A choking sound crawls up my throat, swelling into a scream. I claw at the wound, desperate to tear it out, to be free of it—but hands seize my wrists as thunder rattles the windows.

"Stop, Julian!" my father yells.

Two large male nurses enter the room, restraining me, forcing me back, but I fight, thrash, and scream.

The pain means nothing.

"GET IT OUT!" My voice cracks. "GET IT OUT OF ME!!" I twist, struggle, trying to escape my body, this life—because none of it is mine anymore. Rex is gone! "How could you do this to me?" I sob as they pin me to the bed. "How could you trap me here?" He's gone. He's gone! "And you put his heart in me!" I wail, turning my head to the side and see him standing at the edge of the room.

Towering over the others. Honey eyed. Skin filled with light. He smiles. It's the saddest smile I'd ever seen.

I scream. "WHAT DID YOU DO?" With a bloody hand, I reach for him.

He reaches back.

"REX!"

"Maggie! The oil. Wipe his memory."

"NO!"

"Do it now! We've come too far to lose it all now."

"REX!"

Fingers trace something sweet across my brow. Words are being spoken. The world goes mute.

The silence of deep space is all too quickly replaced by the roar of a monstrous tsunami's approach.

Epilogue

CHRISTMAS EVE 2025

The Coral Sea darkens from its usual crystalline blue to a brooding teal. Swells rise and crash against the reef with growing force, sending up bursts of white spray. Wind bands randomly rampage through the mangroves and palms with a rising, keening cry, thick with the scent of brine and rain, heralding Cyclone Bazza's approach.

Unmoored, he drifts down the beach like a ghost. The world moves on around him, but he feels untouched, a shadow bleeding through the forgotten cracks.

A hollow place now lives inside him. Vast and echoing. An alcove where something vital once shone.

All that remains now is an insatiable gnawing hunger.

An ever burning rage, frozen in perfect stasis.

Just a projection of an angry, impotent boy on a white sheet flapping in the wind.

He sits and gazes out.

After a while, a muted yet deliberate sound approaches. Soft, uneven crunches whisper through the sand, each step slightly sinking before lifting free.

He turns his head to find a little boy and an even smaller girl standing beside him, facing him.

"Why are you out here?" he asks them. "Where are your parents?"

The boy holds a pink hibiscus blossom, the girl a palm-sized clamshell. Their faces light up with bright, carefree smiles as they set their gifts down in front of him. Then, without a word, they turn and dash away, their laughter trailing behind them.

He stares at the pink blossom and the clamshell overflowing with pearls. The blossom pulses with a soft, inner light; the pearls shimmer like captured moonlight. From both, waves of delicate energy ripple outward—vibrant, subtle, and unmistakably alive.

He inhales the effervescent vapours like incense.

The air tastes like sugar melting on his tongue, sweet and electric. The essence touches his skin, seeps beneath it, hums through his chest like a tuning fork. He doesn't just feel it—he absorbs it.

A hush falls. A terrible stillness.

He's not sure how much time passes, but when he comes back to himself, the beach is no longer empty. A multitude of people wearing golden masks have gathered. Not a single voice breaks the silence—only the rhythmic murmur of the deceptive sea.

"Julian," a voice calls from his left.

He turns his head and sees Maggie and Suzannah approaching, their flowing white gowns billowing. Behind them, four masked people follow, also in white.

Everyone is in white, and they all appear to be holding something in their palms.

Clam shells?

"We have tried our best to keep people away while you discover yourself," Suzannah says, kneeling beside him. "But we can only bar the gates for so long. We hope you understand. Some have been waiting decades for this moment."

"I shot Rex," he tells her, bringing his knees up to his chest and wrapping his arms around them. "I can no longer feel him. He's gone."

"Your spirit overpowered his already weakening one," Maggie says, kneeling on his other side. "It was time for him to let go and move on. He was the conduit, but you're the true vessel."

"I'm a vessel?"

"Yes. You are." Maggie's eyes shine bright with fanatical delight. "Now Sylthera can fully integrate with you."

A beat.

"Sylthera?"

"Goddess of Sea and Storm." Suzannah beams.

A pulse.

One by one, voices from the crowd shout epitaphs.

"Mother of Tempests!"

"Mistress of the Tides!"

"Stormbringer!"

"The Thunderous Crash!"

"Maelstrom's Eye!"

"Siren Scream!"

"Harbinger of the Drowned!"

"Angel of the Abyss!"

Each recitation makes him feel tighter and tighter in his skin.

"Sylthera's titles are endless," Suzannah says. "We have worked tirelessly for this day. Hundreds of thousands of hours and millions of dollars."

"Decades of ritual and ceremony," Maggie added. "You should see the receipts. Do you know how many hours I have logged rectifying all those zeros? Tax exemption is not easy, my dear. All the annual reports and returns. Keeping a tight record of income and expenses. And don't get me started on not being allowed to campaign for political or private benefit. But that's over with now because you're here. Fuck world governments, because our queen is now home where she belongs."

Gone was her German accent—poof, vanished. Now she sounds American. Northeastern, even. Connecticut, maybe? If not, her accent was clearly on a world tour with no set itinerary, and absolutely no carry-on limits.

"Your accent…"

"Oops. I love playing pretend. Sometimes just to fuck with people. I hope you're not offended. Nein?"

Nothing's making sense. "You planned all of this?" he asks.

"As you can see by your gathering audience, we are numberless. We see just about everything. We were ready for almost anything. But even we didn't anticipate Rex going so far off the rails, he'd put a bullet in his own face. Where did he even get that gun? I know you homosexuals, darling, but dramatic much?" Maggie gives a theatrical sigh, then turns towards him with a grin sharp enough to draw blood. "Fortunately, your little cardiac episode came right on cue. You were circling the drain, sweetheart—ripe for the taking." She throws her arms out like a deranged game show host. "And just like that, a brand new car. Yay!"

"The White-Crested Fury!"

"Breaker of Ships!"

"Warden of the Depths!"

"The Ocean's Wrath!"

Another woman in a flowing white garment walks around Maggie and kneels in front of him. She removes her mask, and he freezes.

Yvonne? My stepmother!

He takes a breath as she takes his chin with her fingers.

Her gaze is intense.

"Protector of All Who Know Her Rites. Sylthera, Sovereign of the Deep."

A tremor.

"You?" he whispers, the waves crashing louder in his ears, rolling just close enough to kiss his toes. "You…"

Betrayal.

She releases his chin, and he turns his head to see his dad and the Duttons remove their masks.

They are all in on whatever this is.

Deception.

His bottom lip begins to tremble.

Treachery.

"You put his heart in me..."

He has to get away.

"Mother of Pearl," Yvonne calls him, pulling him into her rose scented embrace. The pad of her index finger gliding across his brow and something sweet tickles his nose. "Integration. You are power given flesh. This port is yours now. Protect it from all outside threats."

"What are you talking about?" he asks while also wondering if he can outrun all these masked psychos.

"Hymn in the Howling Winds. Dancer Where Men Drown. Crowned in Foam, Veiled in Wrath."

"Sylthera... Sylthera... Sylthera...."

"I have seen the deaths of millions in the tidepools, Siren Queen. Men, women, and children slaughtered. Their blood turning the tide red. War is coming and we need you to protect these shores."

His voice is as fragile as sea lettuce. "You're insane."

She smirks and takes his hands, pressing them against his chest. Beneath his skin, caged in bone, he feels it—Rex's heart, strong. "Heal thyself, Mother of Leviathans."

His scar is hideous, an ugly reminder that burns and itches in the heat. He hates it. He wants it gone.

She smiles knowingly. "Remove your shirt."

He shakes his head, embarrassed.

"Trust me." She helps him to his feet. "Look."

Making sure no one can see, he hesitates before lifting his shirt just enough to glimpse beneath. His breath catches. With wide eyes, he removes his shirt and hands it to her.

The scar shimmers as a warm glow pulses beneath his skin. Slowly, the puckered flesh smoothes, its injured hue softening to the natural shade of his body, as if time itself is unravelling the wound. Within mere moments, only the memory remains—no traces of an incision, no sign of physical trauma, just untouched skin.

A deep inhale, and the tide surges forward, rushing over his feet. As he exhales, the water recedes, retreating in perfect rhythm with his breath.

"You will never want for anything," she whispers into his ear from behind. "You are loved. You are worshipped. Show them your power, Dreaded Undertow."

A strange, electric heat coils beneath his skin, alive and serpentine, flooding his veins with molten radiance. His bones hum. His blood sings. Power crackles at his fingertips—fierce and undeniable. He lifts his arms to the heavens, not pleading, but summoning. The air bends. The sky listens. Absolute obedience.

The wind stirs once more.

It begins as a whisper—deceptive, reverent—then ascends into a howl, a feral scream that tears through the air like a creature unbound. Above, clouds churn and thicken like boiling tar, spilling across the heavens in roiling waves, devouring light.

The atmosphere collapses inward—dense, crushing, electric with wrath. The air itself quivers, trembling beneath the weight of something vast and starless, something older than the first cave painting. It pulses with a hunger that remembers the first spark that ignited a flame.

Below, the sea goes mad. Waves rise in wild ecstasy, hurling themselves against the reef like creatures possessed, desperate to touch him, to serve him. Then—like titanic serpents erupting from the deep—waterspouts tear skyward, monstrous pillars of ocean spiralling into the heavens.

He breathes in.

And the world fractures.

The sky rips open. Lightning lashes down in white-hot veins, clawing at the earth with furious grace. One bolt strikes so close, it turns the sand to twisted, smoking glass, a black mirror to the chaos above. The thunder that follows is not a sound—it is a reckoning. A divine bellow that splits the air, shatters composure, and drives every soul present to their knees.

There is no running—only the hush of sweet awe, and the exquisite, razor-edge of fear that tastes like honey mixed with the crimson dew of sacrifice.

The waves surge toward him—towering, thunderous, uncontainable.

And he steps upon them.

Not sinking. Not stumbling. But walking—as if the sea remembers its place beneath his feet. The ocean, wild and writhing moments before, flattens under him in reverence, each crest cradling his steps like the bowed backs of servants. Foam spirals at his heels. Saltwind crowns him. His hair grows longer and longer and glows whiter than starlight.

"Sylthera!"

"Sylthera!"

"Sylthera!"

Ah, mouth-watering worship.

"Tempest Unchained," Yvonne cries. "Heart of the Sea!"

He grins—exultant—as spears of lightning hurl themselves from the heavens and kiss his outstretched fingertips. Ivory flesh ignites in radiant fire, and beneath it, his bones glow opaline, crystalline, divine. He is the axis of the storm—lit from within, crowned in fury, sanctified.

Oh, yes.

Unbound from an eon in chains of an equal length.

The storm is awake now—seething, ravenous, free from starry suspension.

He feels Her coursing through his blood like a living tide—an endless current of power surging from Rex's heart, flooding his veins, saturating every cell, bonding with every atom that holds him together.

All heads remain low. They fear meeting the gaze of eternity.

His gaze leers north, the sky darkening so completely that shaman will fumble for a torch, her vision in shadow.

He remembered his promise to make her scream louder than Rex had.

And he will.

His voice will wrap around her like silk and wire—seduction and snare.

He will summon wonders from the deep—things with eyes like lanterns and mouths with concentric circles.

And when he sings—his song of songs—she will come.

She will follow him into the waves.

And there, in the black belly of the sea, the teeth will find her.

And she will be torn apart—beautifully, terribly—note by note. The bloody froth will clothe him.

He laughs as he dances to the melody of the otherworldly voices being carried on the screaming winds.

"We shall drink deep of the infidel's marrow, and when Our hunger is sated, We shall loose tides and ruin upon all who dare oppose Us."

"First Foam!"

"Last Flood!"

"Thunder Heart!"

"Sylthera!"

With a beloved heart full of storm, his eyes fill with gold—ageless, merciless and the sea rises. Beautiful. Terrible. Unstoppable.

The End

Acknowledgements

To the ever-sparkling author and cheerleader, Sandy Davies —

Thankyou from the cores of my frozen, desiccated hearts for being such a steadfast and extraordinary friend. Your sunny words have been a constant beam of light through the clouds, and you mean far more to me than words could ever say.

To Elenore Riley —

I am endlessly grateful for the time, care, and fierce dedication you gave to reading my manuscript and offering feedback that was both sharp and generous. Your friendship and your unwavering sense of justice are treasures beyond measure.

To amazing author Ali Lee —

Thankyou for loving my story from the very beginning and cheering it on every step of the way. That kind of faith is a gift beyond measure.

To the remarkable and fearless author and mentor, Sam Woodgarth —

Thankyou sincerely for guiding me with wisdom, laughter, and generosity. Your insights (and your hilariously well-timed encouragement) have been a beacon on this wild journey towards becoming an Indie Author. I can't wait to laugh with you at our next author talks—it's going to be a riot.

To Nancy Johns —

What a joy it was to meet you at the very first Douglas Shire Book Festival! Thankyou for so kindly agreeing to proofread my manuscript. Your sharp eyes and generous spirit are rare jewels, and I am so grateful. Can I tell everyone about you?

About JB Thomas

JB Thomas is a storyteller in Far North Queensland who thrives on the strange, the spooky, and the delightfully unusual. A proud collector of curiosities, he draws inspiration from ghost stories, folklore, and the dusty corners of history. When he isn't prowling antique shops or chasing after the supernatural, he's spinning MM paranormal romances stitched with eerie twists, heartfelt emotion, and a wicked sense of humour.

These days, you'll often find him at his favourite café, plotting hauntings over a cup of masala chai and a citrus tart (or two). With every tale, JB Thomas weaves a spell that lingers—long after the last page is turned, when you swear you still feel the brush of ghostly threads against your skin.